TO LIVE WITH WHAT YOU ARE

TO LIVE WITH WHAT YOU ARE

Charlie Gracie

A novel

Postbox
PRESS

First published in 2019 by Postbox Press,
the literary fiction imprint of Red Squirrel Press
36 Elphinstone Crescent
Biggar
South Lanarkshire
ML12 6GU
www.redsquirrelpress.com

Edited by Colin Will

Typesetting and design by Gerry Cambridge
e: gerry.cambridge@btinternet.com

A CIP catalogue record is available from the British Library.

ISBN: 978 1 910437 72 8

Red Squirrel Press/Postbox Press are committed to a
sustainable future. This book is printed in the UK by
Imprint Digital using Forest Stewardship Council
certified paper.
www.digitalimprint.co.uk.

what you are

THEY SIT AMONG THE ROCKS under the shore cliffs. Maura's hair swirls in the summer wind. James nestles beside her, perches on the craggy edge. The sky merges grey clouds into white clouds, and sunshine into grey clouds, and the gulls and waders wheel and squeal around them. In the far distance someone pushes a buggy across the sand, head bent into the wind.

Maura climbs down from the rocks and runs, her skirt tight against her bare legs, fast as the wind itself, and she feels it bluster through her and round her as she heads towards the water. Everything inside her sparkles. She breathes the whole world in and breathes it out again. She stops at the water's edge and kicks her shoes off. The person pushing the buggy stops too and watches her. A man, a father, fresh and red-faced in the sea breeze. Maura splashes into the waves, her ankles cold and wet and wonderful.

She stops, breathing hard, the water now up to her knees, seaweed tendrils between her legs. The towns on the far side of the firth are grey-brown smudges, their evening lights flickering orange.

She turns slowly back to the shore. The father is passing, watching Maura in the water; pushes the buggy on quickly. James is still in the rocks. Maura can't see his face, but she knows he is smiling. Suddenly, he is down onto the sand and full tilt towards the water. He arches his run, and Maura starts hers, splashing the straight line towards the man who is now nearly running, and into the shallow spume as she and James arrive kicking and punching in a flurry together, the buggy left and the father fighting, demented, screaming.

The joy, the slowed down joy. Everything working, and James pulling the man down by the neck into the sea salt everythingness of it. His legs flailing.

The smell of the sea inside Maura, the squeal of the oystercatcher, the cry of the baby in the buggy. She struggles to hold the father's legs as James presses his face into the wash. The man kicks, groans in a low voice that seems to come from the sand itself.

The baby quietens to a whimper. The smell of seaweed now, smearing into Maura's face as she squeezes the kicking legs, her hair and the sea in a frantic flurry of feet and bubbles. And then nothing.

A body in the sift of the tide. The ebbing and flow of the broad Clyde. And James kissing her, his lips soft on hers, his tongue, his teeth, his hands holding her gently. Then, she is over him, he is inside her, the wind and the tide washing again and again. Her body on fire.

I: James, man

Random acts of kindness. – A soaking then home for noodles. – Somebody gets what he deserves. – Sleep, sex, sleep. – A very important meeting.

JAMES WENT TO THE Co-op every second Wednesday afternoon. They had lots of fair trade stuff there. Helping everyone out. The way it should be. Nice to be nice.

Nobody he met in the aisles felt the need to breathe down his neck or walk him home and they didn't know his mother and hadn't gone to school with him because the best kind of friend is a friend for a moment when it can't all be washed away and they didn't get impatient and he didn't have to go beyond the doorstep of their lives and they never wanted to come in to his world and they didn't care if they weren't welcome and he didn't either.

He sometimes gave people a secret treat, put a bar of chocolate in their trolley, or a cake or something else nice. He was doing them a favour. And it didn't cost him anything.

Today, in the first aisle, an old man in a blue blazer was leaning onto his shopping trolley like it was a Zimmer frame. He reached painfully up for a jar of stir-in sauce, nudging it slowly towards the edge of the shelf before tipping it into his hand. The old man's skin was red and flaky, all the way from his balding head down to the top of his shirt. Even his hands were reddened and scratched. James had a tiny patch of eczema on his chest and sometimes it itched like buggery. He winced, then skipped to the medicines aisle and picked up a bottle of dermatological shampoo. That would be good. Then he saw a packet of herbal tea bags that claimed to be *all you need for healthy skin and nails*. He chose that instead and went back to find the old man. He was in the toilet roll aisle. James put the packet of tea bags on top of his frozen peas when he wasn't looking. A fat woman with long trickles of brown hair passed him and smiled; she smelled of cat.

The mother with the blonde hair was shopping too, with her son. James was picking a Battenburg cake from a low shelf when the boy pushed their trolley into him.

'Sorry. I'm really sorry.' She pulled the trolley back. 'Sorry about that. Ewan, say sorry to the man.'

Ewan squeezed into his mother.

James's heart pumped hard. He thought about the previous night. What he'd done he'd done for her, for the boy too. There was nothing about her that said she knew. James felt nervous, even though he knew it'd be fine. He tried to remain calm. What would Maura say if she was there? She'd play it cool.

James smiled down at the boy. 'Duznae matter, wee man. Seriously.'

'Sorry.' The boy's voice was tiny.

It was the first time James had heard either of them speak. He smiled at the boy, who squeezed further into his mother's skirts.

'Duznae matter, wee man. Nae probs.'

The woman smiled at him. 'Thanks.'

She had another bruise just below her ear. It was hidden by her hair, but James saw it when she leaned down to cuddle her son into her. He'd known she had a bruise somewhere as soon as he saw her. She held herself in a kind of holding yourself together way, and she was even more attentive to the boy than usual. James could see that kind of thing: pain people wanted to keep to themselves.

She wore it in her walk and in her face. There was something else in her walk too, a kind of confidence, a brashness maybe, mixed with dread. Like something might explode at any moment, but till then she was okay. James smiled to himself. She'd find out soon enough.

He headed to the fruit and veg aisle. He had kept the woman and the boy in his mind for nearly six months, nestled in the corner, his latest project, the one that would finally show Maura what he was capable of. He thought about the Big Fucker's face, the shocked look. James put four carrots in his basket.

The old flaky man was at the till when James headed towards the meat counter. He was talking to the checkout girl as she beeped his stuff through. She had red hair and beautiful deep eyes: the kind of eyes that made James feel warm. He'd seen her a lot and always tried to go to her till because it was a good thing to be near her eyes. It wasn't that he fancied her that much, just appreciated her. He had Maura now, and she was better than a hundred checkout girls.

The old man didn't say anything when the lassie beeped the herbal tea bags through, just carried on chatting. James couldn't hear what they were saying, but she laughed, and the old man look away to the right, then to the left, then down at the floor when she did. His face grew even redder, and he clawed the top of his arm through his blazer.

James walked on to the meat counter, her laugh still in his head. Even though he liked the laugh, and saw the old man all embarrassed but happy, and liked that too, there was part of him that hated them. This was what Maura had done: muddled him up again, just when he was getting good at being straightforward.

When he reached the line for the till, the blonde woman

and her son were in the neighbouring queue. He watched how she ignored the checkout guy, her head down, bustled her shopping into bags and headed quickly for the door. As she left the shop a man raised his hand to wave to someone and she flinched her head to the side, tried to pretend at once that she was saying something to the boy, but she wasn't. And out she went. The boy hurried, skip-and-run, behind her, trying to keep up, and she turned, waited for him. James watched as she stroked his face before the automatic doors closed over and they greyed into the car park.

When it was his turn to beep his stuff through, the red-haired lassie was just finishing and handed over to a fat man with big glasses. He struggled onto the swivel chair.

'Y'awright?' he said.

'Aye, fine.' James hoped he wouldn't say much, felt his eyes and his stomach tighten. The red-haired lassie didn't talk at all really. James liked that.

'That's me on till ten.'

James didn't look at him, but he knew he was smiling and friendly.

'Cannae stand it to be honest.'

James felt his anger rising, but he concentrated on good feelings, nice to be nice.

'Yi just huv to get on wi it. Know what I mean, pal, eh?'

James smiled. 'Aye.' He found himself looking up at him.

'Aye, yir right pal, just need to get on wi it.' The man beeped James's stuff through, his fat smile wide, his eyes bright and dancing.

By the time James had packed his stuff into the pannier, the checkout guy was already onto the next customer. 'Y'awright?'

Outside, the rain had stopped, but the sky was heavy, waiting. A woman in a long blue coat was tying her dog to the frame of the trolley shelter. It was a kind of Jack Russell, one of the ones with longer legs and wiry hair. He stopped to let her finish tying the dog on before unchaining his bike.

The woman turned to James. 'What's your problem?'

'Nothing.'

He shuffled back. He could walk away. Or not walk away.

'Well what you fuckin staring at then?'

Her face was framed in blonde hair and the dog strained towards him, barking. As James stepped back to go round the other way, the woman tutted and fixed the dog more firmly.

'Look what you've done now.'

She was bending, hauling at the dog's lead. Her handbag kept slipping from her shoulder and she swore as she tried to fix it. The dog snarled and the woman became more agitated. Her coat looked like it should be worn on a night out, with big buttons and a belt that had come loose in the kerfuffle. Her shoes were brown and worn, stout shoes as his ma would say, good for your feet. Flat feet and a bad attitude, thought James, as the woman hissed at him. All her pent-upness ready to pop, and she took it out on him. For nothing.

He tried to think good thoughts. He walked over to his bike and looked back. The woman disappeared into the shop, the dog still barking. He could just walk over there and kick it in the ribs, wind the cunt. Kick her too. Right in the chops. He'd done nothing and she started that. Fuckin bastards some folk. His anger rose in a swirl, biting at him to sort it out and not let any fuckin bastardin

arsehole of a wummin or a dug or any fucker fuckin do
that to him.

He breathed in. Then out.

He thought good thoughts.

You are in charge of you.

All that matters is your wee bubble.

Breathe, James, breathe.

You are in a big hula hoop.

Stay inside it.

That was what John the counsellor guy told him.

Don't sort anyone else's shite for them.

Sort your own shite.

Stay inside the hoop.

Leave their shite to them.

He breathed slowly. Saved his energy for other things.
He was better than this, better than her. It subsided, now
like a breeze, almost calm. He could see it was funny when
he thought about it. A mad dug and a mad wummin and
all he was doing was standing back till she got sorted and
he got that for nothing when other times he got nothing
in return. For things he did do.

He felt good about it, kind of. What would Maura do?
She would sort the two of them no problem. Right in the
ribs. He laughed. He would maybe even tell her, and she
would be mad at him for being so nice. And good.

He got on his bike and headed home. It started to rain.
Spits and spots then harder. By the time he'd left the car
park and headed up the hill he was nearly wet through.
The cars *shoom! shoom! shoomed!* past, spraying him
from the dirty road.

When he reached the bus shelter at the top of the hill,
he got off the bike, glad to be out of the rain for a bit.
Incessant. His denims clung to his legs, the damp beginning to seep right inside him. Sucking the heat from his

bones. He looked back down towards the main road. On the left, the street was lined with trees. Cherry blossom, hanging apologetically in the rain. Just inside the park, a swathe of daffodils weaving its way alongside the fence.

Three teenage girls ran past him and jumped the fence into the park. He followed them with his eyes, till they stopped under a cherry tree, trying to shelter under the spindly pinked arms of blossom. One of them turned round. 'What you gawkin at ya weirdo!' He hated that, people always making out that there was something wrong with him, just because he wasn't interested in their stupid worlds. He'd thought when he left school that it would change, but even four years on, they were still there, the numpties who just wanted to have a go. The girls snarled in unison before they merged into one and swept through the rain down the grass, following each other laughing and stumbling into the shelter of the trees at the bottom.

On the right hand side of the street were rows of big sandstone houses. This was where she stayed, the woman with the blonde hair and the boy and the Big Fucker. The houses had grand windows. The gardens tumbled to the roadside, rockeries and shrubs spidered onto the treadworn paths. These were the well-appointed, sought after places.

He jumped the fence to get in among the daffodils. There weren't that many nice ones left, but he picked them anyway until he had a good bunch. He nipped back over the fence, took two elastic bands from the side pocket of the pannier, wrapped them round the stalks and walked into the bus stop.

Some sweet wrappers and crisp pokes that had been swirled into the shelter by the wind were trying to hide in one corner, nestling in with the dirt and twigs. The bench along the back of the shelter was painted blue, but scraped and inked with mentions: *GYTO*; *J loves T*; *Paul*. There were three *fuck the popes* and two *fuck the queens*.

He shook the rain from the bunch of daffodils and placed them near the middle of the bench. They lay there, yellow and green on the blue, waiting for whoever it would be that would take them home, pleased to have made such a daffodil find on such a sodden day. A car door slammed shut on the other side of the road. When he looked up, the woman and her son were walking from the car to the iron garden gate. He was carrying a loaf of bread squeezed in his tiny arms, trudging beside his mother.

James checked the straps on his pannier and got back on the bike. He looked up as he passed their house. She was starting the walk up the wide path. In front of her, the boy, each step a precarious wobbly achievement.

'Good boy.' Each step she said, 'Good boy'.

James cycled past slowly. He smiled, felt certain the Big Fucker wasn't there waiting for her. He couldn't be.

It stopped raining as he hit the downward slope, and in less than five minutes he was at the phone box outside his close. He fished a 10p piece from his damp trouser pocket, put the coin in the space between the phone and the notice board. Just where it could be seen when someone picked up the receiver. That wee coin could mean a lot - a few extra moments to clear the air - or cheer someone up - or anything.

The close was dark and quiet. He bumped the bike up the stairs and chained it to the railings when he got to the door. He'd a job to get the key out, the wet cloth grabbing his hand, not wanting to let go.

When he got into the flat, he kicked the door over behind him and shouted 'I'm home honey!' in a false

American TV voice. He often did that, even though there was never anyone else in.

The smell of the empty house.

He went into the kitchen and undressed, throwing everything at the washing machine. With each step the soles of his feet picked up crumbs and stoory bits from the vinyl floor.

He went back through the darkness of the hall to the bedroom, where he dried off the rain and sweat with a towel and put on some clothes.

He thought about her for a moment. He saw her hair golden and her smile at him and the way she leant over the boy to make sure he was okay.

He put on the radio. The seven o'clock news was just starting, so he listened to the bulletin.

Nothing. He switched it off.

He went back out into the stairwell and took his messages out of the pannier. He put the Battenberg cake just inside the storm doors of Mrs. Carter's flat. Her favourite.

Back in the kitchen, he dumped the rest of the contents onto the table and began to sort them. Milk and cheese into the fridge. Carrots into the press. He left the noodles out – he would have them in a while. He looked at the chops. Two neat slices in a blue tray wrapped in cling film. A logo proclaiming them cruelty free. He tried to imagine what that might mean. Chops from a pig that's *not* been slaughtered?

Maybe not. He put them in the fridge.

He walked into the living room. From the window he could see the city spread out. Alive but silent. He'd loved the flat from the day he moved in, high on the hill, all the world from his window.

The sun was beginning to emerge from behind a huge

dark balloon of cloud. It slanted across the evening sky sending grey flashes from the rooftops. As it fell towards the ragged line of roofs, trees and distant hills, it grew ever bigger and more orange.

A couple of starlings flew up suddenly around the window in a flurry of squawking shrieks and sharp feathers. A bus in the road below hissed to a halt, vomited a couple of passengers onto the pavement and chugged off to the next stop.

He was hungry. He went back into the kitchen and flicked the switch on the kettle before spilling the noodles into a pan. He lit the gas. The yellow and blue of the flame jets hung in unison. They worked so well together, as if there could be no other way.

When the kettle announced it was ready, he poured the water onto the noodles and stirred the worms round and round the pan. He put the chow mein powder in and watched the concoction froth for a moment, then tipped the lot into a bowl.

He wandered through to the living room and turned the radio back on. The room soothed to the strains of a tenor sax, held up by the softwood burr of a double bass and the gentle swish and tumble of brushed drums.

He stood at the window, eating the noodles with a fork from the bowl, looking out into the gathering darkness. The skyline and the clouds were fighting to see which would be first to extinguish the sun.

On the distant motorway, cars began to turn on headlights, so starting the nightly train of eager white lights one way and soft red the other.

He thought about Maura and smiled.

He thought about that Big Fucker. He hated him.

He saw him hitting the blonde-haired woman and the

boy screaming, all of them framed in the grand window, him pulling her by the soft gold hair with his ugly hands.

The previous night, the Big Fucker vague eyed, hateful. Falling home one way then the other in the rain.

'Don't...'

His leering staggering face lolling side to side to side.

'... fuckin...'

He tried to make a lunge at James.

'... do it...'

James pushed him away, and he bounced off the wall right back at him.

'... again...'

James punched him. In the face. Blood.

'... right!'

Him trying to land a drunk fist on James.

He kicked him in the face. Once for all the kicks he'd given her and once for the next time he did it and once because he'd just fuckin had it with the bastardin fuckin bastard and her face sore and the boy screaming. And him. He kicked him again.

The feeling in his foot as it hit his jaw.

Blood on his shoe washed off into the grass in the glistening rain.

The Big Fucker lay there, moaned, coughed, then tried to raise himself. James kicked him again in the body and he rolled down the bank, flattened out over bricks and rubble at the bottom.

His heart beat

Paddum!

Paddum!

Paddum!

High and loud in his chest. The breath rasped hot in his dry throat. The rain soaked into him.

James skiffled down the slope. The Big Fucker laid out on the rubble, his face bloodied and wet with rain. James leaned down to see if he was breathing. Nothing. He grabbed his arms by the wrists and swung him round, the scrape of his body on the stones drowned out by the rain on the trees. He dragged him towards the back of the building, a line of trees and bushes. He moved him round and pushed him under some low-lying shrubs. He tried to listen for breathing. He wasn't sure. He left him there and went home.

The eight o'clock news came on. Still nothing.

James wondered what the woman might be doing just now. He didn't even know what her name was; just thought of her as the mum to the boy. She was probably used to the Big Fucker not appearing, and glad when he didn't.

He imagined that in the morning the police would be calling at her door. She would answer with the boy wrapped round her thigh, and they'd tell her seriously and apologetically and she would cry or stagger or something but inside she would know that it was always going to happen because he was always shouting his mouth off and there was such a thing as a guardian angel and he wouldn't be back any more to batter and humiliate and terrify her.

Maybe, though, James would pass and see him sitting bandaged at the window, and she would bring him tea and stand distant from him. He'd growl his way to fitness and prove his worth again. And she would ache. And the boy would scream. James wished he had made completely sure he was dead.

He opened the window and slopped the remainder of his noodles onto the sill. The birds would eat that in the dawn. The noise of the night crept into the room. The steady hum of rain and cars was interrupted intermittently by someone shouting or the bark of a dog or a horn blowing angry. He looked down onto the street. Groups of two and three people passed in drenched huddles on the pavement, skipping like dancers as cars splashed the puddles in the gutters.

He shut the window again. The sky had merged with the distant hills and James's room had a twin in the outside. He looked at his vague other in the glass. He thought about the boy. Screaming. And him, leaning down with his hands out, and picking the boy up and those hands that can cause such pain being the laughing hands of a father and it could just take an instant and you never know when and you never know why.

He turned and went back into the kitchen. He filled the noodle pot with water and put the bowl in to steep. He was tired, needed his bed; he'd get the pot in the morning.

His ma is laughing in his face. There's not much he can do about it. She's standing on a stick that's pressed over his chest and he can't get up and the breathing is becoming sore. The weight of the stick and her foot is a bird and flies him into the sky, smouldering against the clouds and rising and falling in a fluctuation like the flight of a yellow wagtail on a sunny morning, the sun seeping into the grey of the houses like water into a sponge, the wagtail weaving into the Chapel grounds up and down and up and down till it disappears to a spot in the greenery around the statue of Our Lady. And then she gets up, stretches herself from her concrete base and climbs the wall, the baby Jesus left broken on the grass, and clambers up and into his room and screams in his face with his ma falling back, helpless, falling into the wall, nothing to be done but fall away from the Lady.

He woke up. The sound of a bus. The orange light of the city night.

Later, the sound of the fridge in the kitchen staggering into life woke him again. He swung onto the floor in an easy movement. Like flight sometimes, getting up. As easy as dreaming. The floor was cold, the wood pressing into the skin of his feet as if the only way to stay down was to press up.

He padded across the floor to the pile of clothes and sorted out yesterday's pants and socks from the re-wearable t-shirt and trousers and jersey. The jersey was the green one Maura had bought him. Green with yellow flecks.

He thought back to the Big Fucker. Leering and stupid and drunk. Then down, flat out on the wet ground. He thought about how the woman and the wee boy would have slept last night, half way to perfect sleep because he wasn't there, and half way to Hell because he might turn up at any minute. The door banging to be opened, the Big Fucker like a beast in the orange glow. The boy asleep quiet. She was there to keep him safe.

He got his clean pants from the drawer, blue with the elastic fraying a bit. He stepped into them. He put his socks on and picked up the rest of the clothes.

When he was dressed, he ambled into the kitchen. The clock said 12.55. He'd slept for hours. Maura would be over soon; James's heart skipped. He wondered what he would tell her about the other night. She would be happy. He smiled, washed the bowl he had the noodles in and poured in corn flakes. He usually ate porridge, but today he couldn't be bothered. He still felt kind of full, like the day after a steak. He used to eat rice crispies for a time.

He wasn't sure why because they were just blisters of air, like puffed scabs. He tried to be careful about what he ate, though he was sure the bike kept him fit, burned off all the excess fat, kept him sharp for when he needed to be.

In the living room he put the radio on. The news was just starting and the top story was about a body discovered behind a carry-out restaurant in the city. He knew as soon as they started to speak that it was the Big Fucker.

James felt a rush, his heart nearly bursting out of his chest. He thought immediately about the blonde woman, when the police arrived at the door: the shock, some family member or other arriving over to be with them. Trying to explain to her son. Identifying the body. Avoiding the neighbours' stares and sympathies. And all the time her heart skipping inside, knowing he wouldn't be back.

That was a good thing. Nice to be nice.

The city outside was in full flow, the motorway breathing cars back and forth, busses chuntering in the streets around the flat. The dulled noises of neighbours in the close. He ate a spoonful of corn flakes. Nice and squishy. He preferred them like that. Most people didn't, but he wasn't most people.

Once, when he was seventeen, he had a bowl of corn flakes in a roadside café at Dalwhinnie. It was one of those greasy places that fill you up for a whole day on eggs and bacon and sausage, and everyone that was there was a transient, even the staff, and there was always toast with marmalade. He was hitch-hiking down to Glasgow from Inverness and had been sleeping out in a tent by Loch Ericht. In the early light after a cold and damp night, he'd woken to scraping and voices shouting. At the shore, four men were hauling a big blue canoe from a green estate car down to the water. They didn't see him, packed what looked like a week's supplies into the boat, laughing all the time and shouting the odds to each other.

'You got the coal, big man?'

'You got the Guinness, wee man?'

'Where's ma fuckin jacket?'

They packed the boat up and two of them got in and were pushed down the last of the gravelly shore by the others. As the canoe slid onto the water, the two who were left got onto bikes and headed across the road over the dam. The boat circled a couple of times and set off, the guys paddling in unison.

James wandered down to the edge of the shore and watched them snake into the middle of the loch. One of them was tall with a balding head that caught the early watery light of the sun. The other had a bright red hat on. He could hear them laugh and shout to each other as the wind caught their voices, like a radio that wasn't quite tuned in properly, bits of words floating back across the water. The two cyclists had disappeared quickly across the dam and into the forest on the other side, heads down, going for it. As he turned back to the tent, James saw a rucksack at the front of the car, and it must have dawned on the guys in the canoe about the same time because, as he looked to the water, they were on their way back to shore again.

They were still far out, and he didn't really know why but he started to gather stones and stack them up on the dam road. By the time they were within range, he had about thirty or so, and from that high point could get a pretty good shot at them.

That was really why he had to start seeing John, the counsellor guy who never let his voice raise above floor level. John told him to try to be good.

Stay inside your hula hoop.

To think of the positive, the way he could be better.

What you reap you sow.

James talked to him about his ma and his da and all those kinds of things. John helped him understand why he felt the need to do things like stone two guys in a canoe that he had never met before.

It was fun. The first stone actually hit the one with the red hat on. They were biggish stones, the size you could just hold in your hand. He only got him on the leg, but it was still a good shot. The next two missed completely but he could see they were panicked. He laughed at how they were trying to keep going to the shore but still not wanting to get hit by stones.

Lob.

Weeeeeeeeee!.

Splooosh!!!

'Fuck's sake ya wee arsehole!'

That was it really. Calling him an arsehole. He launched three or four in quick succession and they all hit the boat. One or two must have hit them too because they were shouting at each other now.

'Paddle faster.'

'Fuckin hell.'

James felt free. He threw a few beyond the canoe which really upset them because by this time they were in an inlet so it was almost like they were trapped. Then he hit the big guy on the head. A cracker. Right on the bonce. He was bleeding and curled himself into a ball down off his seat, his pal trying to make sure he was okay and move the canoe away at the same time. James got him on the shoulder and the big guy again on the back. A few missed, but it was still great.

Until he ran out of stones.

The one in the red hat got ashore and chased him.

James could hardly move for laughing, could do nothing when he was grabbed by the hair, kicks into his face. His hair was being pretty near yanked out of his head, but he couldn't fight him off and nothing he could do but try to protect his face. And all the time Red Hat was shouting at him.

'Ya wee...'

Kicked him in the ear.

'...fuckin...'

Twice in the face but his hands took the blows.

'...cunt!'

That one got his nose. He could feel the warm blood on his lip and the metallic taste. A kick in his ribs and another voice.

'Ya wee shite.'

As he looked round he could see Big Baldy running back for another go at him, the blood beginning to stick to his face, but some spattered off his bald head as he ran towards him. What could James do but laugh? Smack! Into his side. He felt a crack and the wind was taken out of him.

Then nothing.

In the distance a dog barking. Other voices raised. When James came to properly, the canoe was gone and an old man was leaning over him, his wife beside him holding onto a golden lab. The dog strained at the leash with its tail wagging, slobbers swinging from the edges of its mouth. The dog's breath was hot and steamy; every pant, a rank blast.

'Should we call an ambulance Ronnie?' The prissy voice grated through the pain in James's head.

'Get that dog to fuck,' said James, his words barely audible above the dog's breathing.

'I think we should, Ronnie.'

'I'm fine. I'll be aw right in a wee minute.'

She was fussing too much. Wanting to be nicey nicey. James knelt up onto his hunkers.

'Lie back down, son, we'll get you sorted.'

James launched at her. 'Would yi shut the fuck up y'auld boot!'

The dog started barking, the old man trying to hold it back by the collar and the woman whimpering and trying to disentangle the dog lead from her arm. James struggled to his feet, took a big deep breath and kicked the dog in the face. As it yelped away, nearly pulling its owners off their feet, James marched off, the pain in his body eased for the time being, back to the tent and zipped it shut and crawled, sore again suddenly, into the sleeping bag.

'Leave me the fuck alone!'

He didn't know how long he slept. There was a blur of the police arriving and packing up and going to the Police Station at Kingussie and getting sent back to Glasgow with his cracked ribs and sore ear and burst nose. No charges. And he still stopped at the café in Dalwhinnie for cornflakes and the all-day greasy breakfast.

When James went to the doctor, she sent him to see John. And John taught him to be good. To do the right thing. Look for the good in himself. On the last day with John, he'd said 'I really feel we've got somewhere James. You've made great progress.'

James kept his head down. Nodded.

'Wipe your eyes, James. You have nothing to be ashamed of.' He handed him a hanky.

He took it from him, wiped his eyes.

Nothing, he knew, to be ashamed of.

Now Maura was teaching him something different. That it didn't matter whether you loved or despised or tormented or acquiesced. The important thing was to be in charge. Of yourself. Of other people.

The radio played Eurythmics *Thorn in my Side*, Annie Lennox blasting out despair in a joyous tone. The motorway buzzed in the distance. He finished the cornflakes and took the bowl back into the kitchen. He put it into the sink, wondered what time Maura would arrive. He felt warm when he thought about her.

The story was at the top of the next two news bulletins. Police were "following a definite line of enquiry". He turned the radio off. Smiled. Big Fucker.

Maura had helped him understand. It was nice to be nice, but sometimes you needed to do the right thing. The best way for you. And not everybody was a talker. Some folk are doers.

When he first held her hand and first kissed her, he hoped they would be together. She said she felt that too but needed to give it time to make sure he was right. There was a spark. She was the flint. He was the tinder.

There was a knock at the door. Maura still knocked, even though he'd given her a key. It was a force of habit with her. But it wasn't her; it was Mrs. Carter from next door.

'Thanks for the bit cake, son,' her hand shaking as she spoke, 'awfy good of yi.'

She always shook like that, a fine tremor that he sometimes saw in her mouth too. She wore the same coat whatever the weather, a blue thing with three different types of buttons where she had replaced them. One of the pockets bulged with hankies and she invariably had one in her shaky hand to wipe away the dribbles when she spoke.

'No problem Mrs. Carter' he said, slowly and loudly in the way he knew she would catch his words. She nodded and headed back across the landing.

At her door, she half turned.

'Terrible news about that Jamieson boy. What's the world comin ti, eh?'

'What's that?'

'Battered an kilt up at the back of Wong's. Tragedy fur that wee lassie all on her ain noo wi the wean.'

He was silent as she undid the door and went into her flat.

'What a shame,' she said, waving the dribbly hanky at him in a final thanks.

Shame? What the Hell would she know. Silly old bat.

He looked at himself in the hall mirror as he swung the door shut. Smiled. Spun all the way round and clapped in a Travolta dance move. Pointed right at himself. 'You,' he moved to the mirror and met his finger at the tip, 'are a murderin little fuck,' and right up face to face and lips to lips, his breath steaming his other self, 'and nobody knows it.'

He stepped back, kept his eyes on himself, smiled, nodded. Maura was right. He was different from everyone else. He did have it in him. He felt alive again.

He went back into the kitchen and switched on the radio. Afternoon music show. He liked it. Good music. *The Killing Moon* was on. He started dancing and singing along.

When the song ended it segued straight into Van Halen and *Jump*. 'Load a shite!' shouted James to the radio and switched it off. 'Load a fuckin shite!' Top of his voice.

A knock at the door.

Maura was smiling at him when he opened it.

'Who were you shouting at?'

She pushed past him, her hair swishing his face, the smell of the outside following her in. She began to unbutton her grey duffle coat.

'Just the radio.'

She laughed.

'Mad boy, have you gone potty or something?' Sorry I'm late, ended up having to stock-take which was a real pain in the neck. Sometimes I could scream.'

Maura never swore. On rare occasions she said *Goodness me* and *Gosh* and *Heck*, but he'd never heard her swear.

'Yi want a cup a tea?'

'That would be good.'

'Still okay to go ti see ma ma the morra?'

'Course, but it'll have to be later. I need to work in the morning. So you and I,' she looked at him with her head to one side and that look in her eyes, 'will have to have a really, really early night tonight.'

'I could do that,' he said. 'Still want your tea?'

'Absolutely. Keep my energy up.'

Tea and sex: the great combo they had discovered. An evening on the couch, snuggled up, listening to the radio and snogging. And drinking tea.

'We're like an old couple in their fifties,' said Maura.

But James liked that. It suited them.

That night, it was the best ever. James felt like the world was his. When they were in bed and naked and together, when he was inside Maura, when her breasts were pressed against him, warm and soft and wonderful, when she went quiet before she came, when her thighs squeezed him like the very life of him would be squeezed out. He felt like the world was his.

'That was amazing,' she said, as they drifted into half sleep and the distant hum of the motorway mixed with the night-time street noises outside the window.

She was amazing. Everything he was tonight and every other day was her.

He smiled. Held her close. 'Love you.'

Then dreamless sleep.

When he woke, Maura was dressed already and eating toast, the smell oozing into him.

Even standing over him, she looked small. Small and neat, always dressed in second-hand shop chic.

'See you at two in the park then. Got to rush. Work to do.'

She kissed him softly, then breezed off. The door of the flat closed, her steps disappearing down the close. He got up and looked out the window, watched her run across the road, putting her hand up to stop a car as she did. She turned back up and smiled. Waved up at him. He wouldn't see her at two of course. She was always late. Brilliantly, beautifully late.

James chilled out on the bench. This was their place, a quiet corner of Kelvingrove Park, tucked in beside the Psalmist, the sculpture that witnessed their kisses.

The park was quiet, just the way he liked it. Where anything could happen and nobody would know. Maura knew the things he knew: the sound of derision; the snide look; the laugh of the sheep who follow the leader. He and Maura didn't ever follow but.

The leaves on the ash trees behind The Psalmist were peeping from the grey bark, bursting through the black-eyed buds. The birds were cacophonous. In front of him, the path snaked through pale shrubbery and disappeared into the wider spaces of the park. The brown stalks of winter were beginning to be swamped by the rush of spring. The disappointment of the fresh start upon them.

He waited.

The air was soft with the cold nip of March. The clever month of renewal, folding winter into a drawer till next year, scraping the last of the frost away and greening everything in readiness for the summer. March was the butcher, skinning the earth, snapping joints and selecting cuts in readiness for the cooking and eating. And then what? Eating and drinking till they were full. Eating and drinking and shitting and hungry with disappointment. All for nothing really. Maura knew this. He knew this.

'It's like there is only ever a door between us,' she said once. A door. You could put your face to it, feel the warm wood on your cheek, sense the breath from the other side, like your own breath in a dream.

The weather forecast said sunny. It started to rain, to drizzle really. The smir soothed him, fell soft onto his skin, cooled.

He was cool about Maura being late. That was how things were with them. No big pressure. If she was there she was there. If he was there he was there. They didn't kill each other with love or guilt or hassle. Just being happy together when they were, and chilled when they were not. He would like to be with her all the time of course, but he knew that if you clawed at someone, they would disappear.

The first time James saw Maura, it wasn't the tone of her eyes or the colour of her hair that got him, but the calm way she ruled the space around her. Like she knew what it was to be in charge. Without a fuss.

In the stepped semi-circle at the Clydeside, he was

eating his piece among the other lunchtimers. Sitting on the stone steps in the sunshine, watching.

His job as an assistant technician with the Lothian Partnership was only just tolerable. Mostly doing the donkey work for the technicians and the architects, who of course were paid loads more than him. But that didn't bother him. He didn't need much to live on. Drew his belt in when need be. The office was high up on the top floor above George Square and the ancient lift to get there was operated by an alcoholic who lived in an attic flat.

In the city centre, the buildings stuck their chests out, vied with each another, squeezed into their patches of earth. He could hide forever in the city if he wanted, drift among people, smell them, looking into them, seeing what they did. Sometimes he followed one person, usually before work, until they went into a building. Didn't do anything, just followed them. He could disappear into the grey stone the same way he used to disappear into his woods. Melt into the city rain. Merge into all the faces. Nobody. Nothing. He was better now. More in control.

If it was rainy at lunchtimes, he went to the Stirling Library, pored over old maps. He loved looking at how the Monklands were far flung only ninety years before, now scooped up by the hungry city. He roamed far into the spread of Perthshire, from Athol down to Callander and to the snaky Forth.

On sunshine days, he sat with everyone else on the steps. The riverside was being transformed; someone had caught a salmon up towards the Falls of Clyde, the first for forty years. The steps were part of a new walkway that had begun to creep along the bank of the river, even sneaking under the bridges at the Broomielaw. The broken glass was being swept up and the shiny concrete of the walkway shouted the new Glasgow, miles better, Mr.

Happy popping up everywhere. The river was still brown, but, and there was still a smell of pish in the corners.

Then Maura arrived, sitting herself across from him on the other side of the semi-circle. The day a fight broke out between two blokes. One of them wore a suit and square-edged shoes. The other was a smaller, quiet looking guy with a big Icelandic jersey. They suddenly erupted in a flurry of fists and half-eaten sandwiches. The crowd parted as the two ran down, into the middle, half gladiators, half clowns. Some people stood up immediately and ran away, spilling back into the street above. A few others circled round, not knowing what to do. Three guys and a lassie in a sharp suit jumped onto the combatants, tearing them off each other. A few on the outer ring at the top of the stairs were laughing, nudging each other, pointing down before turning away.

James didn't move. Watched the whole thing unfold.

Maura. Sitting on the opposite arm of the semi-circle, the only other spectator who could see the drama for what it really was.

She'd been reading a book. James had noticed her even before the fight. There was a glow about her. He knew as soon as he saw her she was someone special. She had a solid grimness that created an aura around her. She sat on the stone step, watching.

James saw her eyes sweep up from under her fringed brown hair and catch it all. When the flurried fight ended, his eyes met hers. She lowered her head slowly, not taking her eyes from his till she disappeared behind her fringe and back into her book. Nothing else.

She had tuned right in to the fight, he could see that; she enjoyed the moment, could feel the thinned humanity of everyone there. Joy in a slice of malice, like lemon in gin. It was the malice that gave the edge. Blood in the veins.

He smiled at her, but she was into the book already and he took his eyes back to his piece, started eating again. When he looked up, she was on her feet, setting off up the steps. She didn't look back. He threw the end of his piece and cheese to the seagulls and followed her as she strode on up through Saint Enoch's Square and into the art shop off Argyle Street. Her head up, her strong, definite footsteps marking the rhythm of the street, her hips swaying, her head aloft.

After that, she crept into a corner of his mind and sat there. When he went back, on that first day, to the stupid office, she was with him. She said nothing, but he knew she was there. And nobody else knew it.

She'd been wearing a baseball jacket, an old-fashioned one with red flashes on the shoulders, and faded jeans, and a bright blue tee-shirt with some kind of tree on it. He'd thought it was the very dab. He told her that soon after, before he could confide in her the real first impression: that she was all of a sudden his reason to breathe in the morning.

Maura laughed later about him stalking her, the days he pitched up at the art store, hanging about like a sad case, looking away every time she glanced across from behind the counter at him. He tried to pretend he was looking at the wee blocked printy things for making shapes on card, or the screeds and screeds of coloured paper, but after two weeks, when he appeared every second day for the whole of an elongated lunch break, she spoke to him.

'Can I help you at all?'

She had a soft English voice that almost smelled of the moorland.

'Naw, just ... lookin.'

'Look then, but you might actually want to buy too.'

'Okay, then.'

And he left without saying anything else. It was another three weeks before they found themselves together again on the semi-circle of cold grey steps. James was more aware of rising from the crowd, and, when she threw him a crumb of a smile, he steeled himself to think that at some point he might talk to her properly. Like a key that unlocked him.

The next week, and he was on the steps by the river again, eating a roll and chips from the Cottage, when she sat next to him. She just appeared and when he looked round, she was staring at him. From about three spaces away. He could feel her there even before he saw her.

'Hi,' she said

'Hya.'

'Did you ever buy those pencils?'

A wee bit of a nip, then softer.

'You come here quite a lot.'

'Aye,' he replied, 'I come for ma lunch break.'

'Me too.'

That was it. The big introduction.

She was Maura, worked 'as you obviously know' in the art store. She was there till the autumn to go back to the Art School and do a post graduate in sculpture, sculpting in steel and stone. She thought his job in the architect's office was 'interesting' but almost immediately agreed with him that it was dead and boring and that he was right to be looking for a job in a museum. She hoped he'd get it. Every time she spoke, he felt her burn into him. Alive.

The skies greyed as they talked, and the rain spilled, scattered almost everyone else clattering back to their offices and shops. They sat in the downpour till they found themselves heading along the walkway to the girdered railway bridge. They stopped in front of a statue that faced out over the river from the top of a high metal plinth. La Passionara, Dolores Ibarruri, stood with her fists to the sky.

Maura suddenly burst into life, spinning rain-soaked and wide-smiled and shouting the words on the plinth – *better to die on your feet than to live forever on your knees* – spinning in the wetness and the concrete and the steel of Dolores and the railway bridge shunting out over the Clyde above them, the starling grey and iridescent sky alive with the sweep and swoop of the city's noise, its voice rising on the wind, twisting round the buildings and the bridges, the diesel smell of the air throwing itself from river to soggy street, Maura all the time in her spin, laughing the rain away, her eyes a flash every time she spun round to him.

It was then she first kissed him, that he felt her breath in him, her breasts against him soft through their coats, that he first knew her waist in his arms, her neck and her hair on his fingers.

Dolores Ibarruri stood on her plinth above them, her steel stare directed across the river.

James stood and turned to the Psalmist. The Psalmist stared back and said nothing. James walked down to the edge of the Kelvin, into the shade of the trees. The arch of the road bridge was dark and wet and covered with ivy and the deep green of mosses. A heron flopped into the shallows, looking for prey. James smiled: a quiet place, where anything could happen, un-noticed.

Back to the bench, he saw Maura coming though the big park gates. Her beautiful smile, her teeth happy and white, her hair back in a ponytail, her neck pale and enticing. She was wearing a bright red coat.

She bounced down beside him. For a moment, she didn't say anything, only looked up at the sky and squeezed his hand.

'I'm looking forward to meeting your mum you know.'

'That's good,' he said, thinking on one hand that she must be mad and on the other that this was the girl he would always be with.

They'd been building up to this for weeks. Maura and his ma. James had tried to explain to Maura what it might be like, that his ma could be more than a bit awkward, that he'd never taken a girl home before, and while a lot of the reason was that he had never actually had a girl to take home really, part of it was that he'd never take just any girl to see his ma. She would have to be made of strong stuff.

They were on the bus. James was quiet and Maura asked was he nervous about the visit. Maybe; but it wasn't only that. He wanted to tell her about giving that Big Fucker what he deserved and how she'd helped him see it was a good thing.

If you wanted it to be.

'Be yourself,' she said, all the time.

It would wait till after they'd been to see his ma.

Maura squeezed his hand harder. 'See that guy you were telling me about last week,' she said.

'What guy?'

'The one that hits his wife and his son and you always say it reminds you of your dad.'

'Aye?'

'It's not right, is it? That he just gets away with that.'

'Naw.'

He jumped up.

'C'mon, this is our stop.'

He chapped the door of the house and opened it. He shouted in. No reply. The smell of bleach in the hall was strong today, which could either be a bad thing or a good thing. He looked round at Maura, held his nose. She crinkled hers back at him.

He showed her into the front room. The television was on low and classical music drifted into the darkened room. A good sign.

'You sit there and I'll tell her we're here.'

His ma was in the kitchen, standing at the sink with her back to him. Whistling.

'Hya'

'Hi son,' she replied, not turning round.

'I've brought Maura ti meet yi.'

'That's good, son.'

'D'yi forget?'

She stopped what she was doing and half turned. She didn't speak for a few seconds. James held his breath.

'No.'

She turned round and held her hands out towards him, yellow rubber gloves dripping water onto the floor.

'Just getting this finished before I say hallo.' Barbed. 'That okay with you?'

James breathed out slowly, his stomach churning. 'Aye.'

She tutted and spun back to the sink. She was washing dishcloths in bleach. James decided not to hurry her up; it would only annoy her.

'I'll go and tell Maura to come in.'

'No you won't, son, you just sit there and I'll go in a minute.'

He knew better than to argue.

II: Maura, woman

A decision made and tested. – Locking horns. –
A brother remembered and secrets shared. – Music in
the night air. – Consummation.

THE VOICES ON THE STREET rose and faded. Maura held her breath. And everything – every single thing ever – beat into her. There, on the edge of the river, with James smiling at her. They were silent. Unseen.

What is the difference, she wondered, between what a man is when he does this and what a woman is? What a man feels and what a woman feels?

Things used to seem clear, before her mum died. When what Maura saw a woman do, and what she saw a man do were ordinary, in the sense that they were shared by all women or all men, pretty much. There was no more thought about it than breathing. Even after Paul died, she didn't feel that this was her as a girl or a woman that felt and planned and did things; but just her. Maura.

But now, in this moment, on the rainy spring side of the river, she thought very much about it. What it meant to be a woman. To her. What it meant to be a man. To James.

She looked up the grassy slope to the street. They were hidden partly by the dark, partly by the rain, partly by the leggy spindles of willow trees. The shouting and the foot-steps that had made them hold their breaths splattered by, thinning out to the main drag and towards the bridge to the city centre, mingled now with the other unknowing, unseeing night-timers.

The day had started in a bright blast of sunshine. She'd finished her work earlier than expected and then rustled in the second-hand shop in Ruthven Lane for something appropriate: not too pushy, not too demure. She was going to meet James's mum for the first time and she wanted to let her know that there would be no quarter. She hoped James was wrong about the two of them not getting on, but she had to prepare for battle if battle came. The red jacket did it.

Things were going really well with James, not only loving him, which of course she did. Already. But him. He was better for her being there; she could see that. She could feel things move inside her. She was ready to put her weight behind her and James. Together.

When he'd asked her to go and meet his mum, he seemed to crumble, almost immediately pulling back.

'Mibbe it's no that good an idea when I think about it.'

She told him, 'Be yourself James, be what you really are.'

'It's easy wi you Maura. I know yir probably right, but I'm still trying ti get there maself.'

She was angry when he told her about all the changes he had made and how he was still drawn to being "a better person", as he called it. She was sad too, because this wasn't what he really was, a good and shiny person. He had a different good and shiny that he had buried. But she was still hopeful; she'd seen it glimmer in him over the last few weeks.

He really did frustrate her at times and a part of her still worried that she might be wrong about him: one minute he seemed to retreat to his false self and the next rose out of that into what he really was and would become.

It was that first night when they'd walked to the Kelvingrove Park, away back in the autumn, that she'd told him this. Maura was ready for him to leave at that moment and never come back. She'd chased boys away before, and she knew that she had to test them early to make sure they were right, to make sure they had the balls to be with her. All this talk about doing good to strangers, and forgiving everyone else for the things they did, was rubbish. 'Bullshit', she'd said to him, and that was nearly that. It took a lot to make Maura swear.

James looked into the sky when she said it. 'I don't know that it is bullshit Maura... I'm happier now than I was... happier being a good guy than a bad guy. Happy that I'm trying to be part of a better life.'

He'd walked off, then turned and came back. 'Are you for real?'

'Yes, James, I am for real. Are you? I can see what you really are.' She held him firmly by the arms. 'I can see it in you, right away inside you.'

She'd looked into his blue grey eyes and there it was: the need to make it happen for yourself, and not just witness it or read about it or see it on the telly.

James had taken a long time to come to the understanding that he and she were the same and that for them to be together he would need to go back to what he had been before. That he needed to unearth himself again. That he needed to re-do what was undone.

He left her, not then, but three weeks later, as the first chills of October were setting in. He didn't contact her again till the snowdrops were well on. She'd almost given up on him. She thought he was another one she'd misjudged and, even though she felt more deeply more quickly for him, she'd begun to let him slide from her mind. She threw herself more and more into her sculpture. She had begun to fashion her style, to work the metal and stone into pieces of energy and force that began to attract interest beyond the Art School folk who already knew her. It was as if that late autumn was a gestation period, that James had fertilised her work with his presence. She knew, in the rare moments that she consciously thought about him, that he was still real and separate, but he existed with her in the swings of her hammer and the flames of her torch and the sharp edge of her chisel.

She knew she couldn't make him something he was not, that she couldn't change him. But she felt deep inside that she could help him to be what he really was. All the potential of an un-worked piece of steel. Or a slab of Kilkenny limestone. A reality inside that only needed shaping.

In the few weeks since he'd had come back, it was intense. She'd decided to give him one last chance to get it right, and, even though he wasn't yet there, she was hopeful.

She worked most nights sculpting, and squeezed precious time with James around it. Her art became more focussed. When other people saw flawless nobility in a raw object, Maura saw a child cowering; when they saw a cowering child, she saw a strident, arching beast. She could touch the essence of things in a way other people never could.

Mostly what she saw inside a thing was strong and fierce. In her workshop space, her corner was darker, pulsing deeper down than the others, and the metal work she was developing was rasping and hungry and disturbed everyone who came across to watch her bash and weld and bend the metal sheets into her figures. Her row of five children beaten down by an unseen thing; a mother whose arms reached hopelessly to save a child from an unseen thing; the male figure she worked on now whose head twisted away from his torso, his face lit up as it looked towards some unseen thing.

The unseen thing was always there, stage left, the true centre of her art, the thing that must have somehow driven her forever and avowedly drove her now. Her love for James, bubbling inside her was no less part of this than the disdain she had for most of the people around her. Her malice towards others was equal to the love she was now allowing herself to share with him. She knew she needed him.

To get to James's mum's, they caught the bus to Baillieston, driving from the city centre past the run-down area around the Barras market and into Parkhead and Shettleston. She didn't know this part of the city well. She lived in the west, where things looked brighter. It suited her to live a short bus or tube ride from the city centre because she could be among people there and never be known; she could enjoy the dark corners and the chase when she wanted.

At Shettleston, a group of men were gathered on a street corner, drunk. One of them, fat and unstructured, gestured with his fist when he saw James looking out. He stood up unsteadily and shouted something that looked like "wanker". James laughed and gave the *come ahead* sign with his hands. The men, suddenly energised, lurched towards the bus and rattled on the windows, shouting they were 'Goany fuckin kill you ya wee dick!' James was cool. Nodded back to them. Laughed. He looked away as they continued to pound the windows till the driver sped off. She kissed him on the cheek and he just nodded again.

'You know Maura, I've been thinking about what you've been sayin. Mibbe I'm more like you than I thought. I've been kiddin maself on.'

She turned his head round with her hands, right round till he faced her, still the trace of a smile on his face, and she kissed him full and hard, her tongue just touching the edge of his lips, and a rush through her body that made her skin feel like it was buzzing, like every time she moved her lips harder to his, or her tongue touched his lips she felt she could have lifted off and flown.

When they got to the start of Baillieston, he jumped up and ran to the front.

'C'mon. This is our stop.'

She followed him, the bus beginning to move just as she stepped onto the pavement. She couldn't see him anywhere. As the bus took off she looked after it and across the road and round in both directions. There was a hedge alongside the road where they had alighted, so she peered through it. Nothing. She started walking, almost automatically, in the direction the bus had travelled. Then a voice from the other direction hollered, 'Maura! Maura!'

'Idiot,' she said to herself, and looked round to see James's backpack standing against a sycamore, about fifty yards down the road. He stepped out from behind the tree and smiled to her.

When she reached him, she slapped him on the arm.

'Idiot,' she repeated.

'Ithiot,' he mimicked and laughed. Ran round to the back of the tree and stood there. She could hear his breathing.

She tried to be angry but found she couldn't keep it at the right level, so she ran round the tree and hit him on the arm again. He laughed and she laughed and they looked each other in the eyes for a moment and kissed again. Soft now. Soft and for a long time. It was like the first time they'd kissed under the Passionara in the rain. It had been hardly any time since then and here they were, going to see his mum. Here she was in love with him.

Sometimes James seemed really young, even more than the three years' difference. Like now, when he was acting the clown. But she still knew deep inside he was right for her. And that they would be together.

'Mon we'll walk up through the park,' he said. 'Bit of air an that.'

They walked along the streets, the houses here leafy and gardened and neat looking. When they reached the entrance to the park, they passed swings and a small slide that sat beside a derelict, boarded up building. Beyond, a huge slope disappeared up through tall trees. James led her up the path that ran at a diagonal across the slope and up to a broad raised circle of grass at the top.

'This is where I used ti sit,' he said, looking up into the branches of one of the beeches.

'I spent most of ma time on ma own, but sometimes I used ti come here wi ma pals. That tree was mine. I was the only one that could climb it. Used ti sit up there for hours listening ti aw the dafties talking shite.'

He looked up into the high branches. Like he was lost in it.

Maura looked out over the city. High-rise flats spiked the greying skyline to the west. The houses nearest them were surrounded by green, but as she looked just beyond, it was roofs with chimneys and television aerials sprouting, and the dimming of the sky and the threatening rain. The wind rose and a cool smell like dead leaves floated in it.

'Mon,' said James, 'we'd better no be late or she'll go aff her nut.'

He always spoke about his mum like this, as if she were a dragon or a jailor and Maura was unsure if it was real or just how he saw it. When he'd told her about his counselling and how he'd tried to change, she saw in his eyes something that told her that he was waiting for someone like her to come along and help him get really strong again, to tell him it was all right to keep alive the feelings and thoughts he'd tried to suppress. All right to stand up to his mother.

'I'm quite looking forward to meeting your mum, James. I'm sure we'll get on fine.'

He shook his head, squinting a smile. 'I told yi, she's a bit funny. And I don't mean funny ha ha.'

'I'll be fine James, don't worry. I can handle anyone.'

'I'm sure yi can, but you've no met anyone like ma ma.'

As they passed out from under the trees and down towards the gates of the park, the first big spots of rain began to fall.

They ran from the shelter of one tree to the next and the next, the bare branches only stopping the rain for a moment before it spat through. James sat down at the bole of the last tree that rose just at the gate out of the park and rustled two plastic bags from his backpack. He handed a Co-op one to Maura. She looked at it and then at him.

'What am I meant to do with this?'

She watched as he fitted his Fine Fare bag onto his head and twisted the loose end round and round, then tucked it firmly inside the plastic hat he'd made.

'Just wrap it in a wee bit and it'll fit,' he said.

Maura laughed.

'You must be off your head James. Do you really think ...?'

She stopped when she realised that he did think that she should, in fact, walk along the road with a plastic bag on her head. But when she thought about it, it made perfect sense. She'd keep her hair dry, and who would see her? And what did she care anyway? James helped her with the mechanics of it, and they skipped quickly together as the rain fell.

They ran and ran in the rain past the gardens and driveways till her heart was bursting in her chest, James dragging her by the arm shouting, in that high pitched way, 'Run like a couple a dafties!' She laughed, nearly fell three times. James did fall eventually, almost taking her with him, as they reached a row of old buildings, broken and boarded up, the sandstone damp and un-cared for, the guttering split and spewing rain water onto the pavement. James stood for a second when he got back up, breathing and gasping and laughing and soaked through. The Fine Fare bag was still tight on his head, the water running off it and down his face. Maura had to wipe the rain from her eyes every few seconds, the *batter batter batter* on the plastic bag was driving her mad.

'Is it far?' She gasped.

'Naw, just over the road.' He pointed to a block of squat two-storey flats on the other side of the junction. A bus sloshed past, spitting water from a puddle towards them; it missed, but they were so wet it wouldn't have mattered much. Maura wondered how good her red coat looked with the plastic bag hat.

A small girl arrived, skipping wetly from the road that ran up from the right. She wore Wellington boots and a short grey skirt and a blue diamond-stitched anorak with the hood bedraggling behind her. The whole girl dripped as if she were made of rain. She had black black hair and she stopped when Maura turned to look at her. The girl stared from among her wet straggled hair with eyes that were so blue Maura could almost not bear to look at them. So blue they could slice through a person. Maura looked away and nudged James to see her too. He turned to the girl and shouted, 'Fuck off ya wee bitch!' as loud as he could. The girl stared for one second more and ran back the way she had come, down the road into the rain.

James laughed. 'That told her, eh?' He bent down and gave Maura a kiss on the lips, the wet of the rain nearly melting their mouths together.

When they stopped, Maura looked at him and smiled. He smiled back, his mouth wide, 'Bet yi didnae expect that, did yi?'

'No, James, I did not.' she replied. 'Quite not like you at all'.

She squeezed his hand tight.

They crossed the road, still holding hands, and James led her into the first gate and up the concrete steps at the side of the building. It was grey, rain-stained roughcast with a green stain running down from the apex above the door. Inside, a set of stairs ran up to another door.

James turned to her. 'You sure about this?'

'Of course, stop going on.'

Maura was sure, but a slight flutter ran across her chest. The inside stairs had a bleached smell about them and there was a pale green carpet that ran to the top. Maura guessed James's mum had been cleaning for their visit, a thought confirmed when he opened the door and his shout of 'Hya Ma!' was met with another, stronger waft of bleach. The smell blew out into the yellow-painted stair-well and Maura coughed as it hit the back of her throat.

'Sorry, shoulda warned yi about the mad cleansin thing that she does when somebody's visitin. At least it means that she's lookin forward ti meetin yi.'

'No problem James,' Maura replied, feeling simultaneously pleased at his explanation and worried about how unkempt she was looking for this woman who'd been scrubbing and cleaning all morning for her arrival.

They entered, still dripping rain, into a dark hallway. James led her into a large square room, lit only by the television and a dim table lamp beside the closed heavy red curtains. A radio was playing quietly. At first Maura thought that the music came from the television till she realised that the programme was horse racing and that the piano music didn't fit. James motioned for her to sit.

'I'll be a wee minute. Ma ma's in the kitchen.'

He disappeared back out of the room.

Maura tuned into the music. She recognised it as Chopin, breezy, but focussed and serious under the surface. She thought about what James had told her about his mum and dad, the stories of fierce violence, his dad's death that he had always thought was his mum's doing, all the things she did and said to him. Maura felt a wave of anger at James's mum and fantasised about running into the kitchen, grabbing her by the hair and punching her ten times in the face. Her fists clenched and her stomach tightened and her heart beat loudly.

James hadn't come back after fifteen minutes. And not after twenty. Suddenly, through the door she came, James's mum and no James with her. She was a tall woman, taller even than James and she'd the same angular face and tightness in the way she walked. She wore a pair of black leggings and a long bright red cardigan, darker than Maura's jacket. Her hair had been dyed dirty blonde and was pinned neatly back with a wisp floating free on one side of her face. She came over to Maura, took her hands and sat down beside her.

'So you're the lassie that's stole ma boy's heart then, eh?'

She cupped Maura's hands in hers and squeezed gently. Maura smiled, didn't really know what to say.

'That's right Mrs. ...'

'That's enough of the Missus you, ma name's Ellen and yi call me that or nothing.'

'Right. Ellen.'

She smelt of alcohol and cigarettes. And bleach.

She looked into Maura's face, right into her eyes and said, 'I like you, hen. But you'd better be good ti ma boy or,' she smiled, 'I'll do yi.'

She sat for a moment and held Maura's gaze without flinching. Maura looked straight back at her. Unflinched also. Then Ellen moved her eyes back to Maura's hands.

'That's that oot the way then.'

She rose up, placed Maura's hands down onto her lap and stood back from her. Before Maura could react further, Ellen continued, 'Yi wantin tea? And a wee biscuit? Mon you through wi me ti the kitchen.'

She yelled ahead. 'James, huv you got that tea sorted yet, son?'

Out Ellen went, looking back to summon Maura with her.

Maura hesitated, watching her as she strode out of the room. She took a deep breath. Better, she thought, to leave it there, to give Ellen the upper hand if that's what it took. Maura felt strangely at ease: she'd planned her attack on James's mum for weeks, ever since he'd begun to tell her about all the things that happened to him, planned what she'd say, how the old bat would feel when Maura shrivelled her with a few sharp words. But there was something about Ellen she liked. Her straightforwardness. The same look in her eye as James had. She pushed the feeling of disloyalty aside and followed her into the kitchen.

The kitchen was even darker than the living room. A small square table covered in a faded yellow cloth sat in the middle, with two white-painted chairs, and there were plants on almost every other surface. James had his back to her as she entered the room. He turned round in the half light and smiled a watery kind of smile that was as half lit as the house itself.

'Right, baw-heid, get that tea made fur me and Laura.'

'It's Maura, Ma, no Laura ...'

'Sorry hen ...'

'Godsake.'

'Don't you go Godsaking me boyo.'

'Right, Ma.'

James caught Maura's gaze and raised his eyes to the ceiling. Maura had never heard a mother talking to her child like that before. She wondered for a second what her own mum would have been like now if she was still alive, if she would have grown beyond all the pain of her life, or if she'd be a bit like Ellen, living in the semi-shade. She smiled at James and he returned only a glimpse of a smile before reaching through a trailing spider plant into a cupboard and getting out three mugs.

Ellen sat Maura down at the table. James emptied a packet of fig rolls onto a plate and brought them over. There were two teapots, a chintzy pink one that Ellen poured her tea from, and a stainless steel one for Maura and James. Ellen launched nearly at once into stories about things that James had done when he was a boy, laughing at her own jokes and smoking one cigarette off the other. James stood quietly most of the time, his back against the sink.

Ellen wasn't quite the witch Maura had expected. She was funny: both kinds of funny. After the initial word of warning, she seemed almost kind, complimenting Maura on her coat and how nice her eyes were and telling James he was 'a lucky wee bugger ti huv a lassie like this one, all proper spoke and that.'

Maura had rarely been in a house in a place like that. Boroughbridge was nice, in the slightly boring sense, but peaceful. The area around Ellen's house was alien to Maura, with broken fences, and smashed glass on the pavement. The house itself was tired, not in a shabby chic way, but in a done-in way. When Maura was young, her mother often took her and her brother Paul to visit Great Aunt Tilly. Tilly lived in a tiny cottage adjacent to a farm in the Pennines. Her house was dark and unyielding like Ellen's, but dustier, and with no bleach. Everybody else that Maura grew up around seemed to be happier than Great Aunt Tilly. Maura learned as she grew that she and her mum and dad and Paul were very nearly ascendant, unstuck, with futures just there in the foreground. All that changed, of course, when Paul died, but the seeds were there and Maura had moved on, to Art School and Glasgow and a future just around the corner. She could see from Ellen's kitchen and James's shrunken-ness in it, that everything there was more fixed, more likely to be inevitable.

Hardly a word from James the whole time. He washed the dishes that were lying in the sink while Maura and Ellen talked. Maura watched his eyes flit from one to the other and back as they spoke. He seemed on alert, an animal waiting to pounce, or flee. Ellen moved from stories about James's childhood to prodding Maura about her own life. She burst into a laugh when Maura described her sculptural work, and even when James *Godsaked* she didn't stop, not even to rebuke him. Maura didn't understand what was so amusing, but she let it go. Ellen offered another fig roll each time Maura finished one and by the fifth she slowed down to a nibble for fear of getting a sixth.

James continued to stand, one minute staring at them as they spoke, the other tidying. He put the dishes in the stand to drip before drying them with a new tea towel from the drawer. Back into the cupboard, wipe the surface, empty the basin, dry it out. Maura felt she knew him better as Ellen spoke more about things he did as a boy and laughed and drank her tea. She imagined him there, in that house, scurrying away from the violent outbursts, his dad's bad-handedness, his mum's crazy exuberance. Maura's anger weaved in with pride that James had undone so much of all that, and delight that something had led him to her. She knew, looking around the dark life that Ellen had, that this was what made James James. This was what was needed for him to make Maura happy. Part of her wanted to slice Ellen's head off; the other wanted to hug and kiss her in gratitude.

James sorted the three apples and a tangerine that sat in a glass bowl into different configurations; he wiped the surface of the chopping board and shuffled the various plants into a semblance of order. The more Ellen talked and smoked, the more tea she drank from the chintzy pink teapot. The smell of bleach and smoke was soon competing with the smell of vodka.

Suddenly, Ellen launched at James, 'Fuckin idiot!' She shoved the seat back and was in his face. Maura was so taken aback at first she didn't respond. James did nothing either, only held his mum's gaze.

'Would yi fuckin look what yir doin!'

At that, Maura felt the rush of energy through her body. She sprung up and stood in between them, staring, not saying a word, fists clenched, up into Ellen's face, Ellen staring right over her at James, her vodka breath permeating the whole moment.

James whispered calmly in Maura's ear. 'It's fine, she'll be aw right in a minute.'

Sure enough, in not even a minute, Ellen was all right, backing away from Maura, eyes still on James. 'Aye, yi'd fuckin better no.' And then down, back into her seat.

Maura stood in the middle of the kitchen, her heart pounding. James was back to tea-towelling the worktop and moving the plants about.

'I was just sorting the plants fur yi Ma, it's fine.'

Maura looked at them both. They were like dogs after a violent flurry, edged into their new places in the order of things. Lines drawn and re-drawn.

Then lightness, the breath of the moment let out. James shook his head when Maura looked up at him. Smiled that beautiful wide smile of his.

Ellen poured herself more vodka tea, drank it down and then stood upright again. She banged the table and announced in a shrill loud voice, 'Right!' She was up and striding out of the kitchen. 'No harm to either of yous, but I need ti get on and yous'll need to be goin too no doubt.'

And, with a quick flash of a tight smile back to Maura, 'Lovely ti meet yi, hen.'

James followed her. Maura watched them disappear together into the darkness. She couldn't hear what was said. He reappeared a few moments later, pensive.

Ellen shouted back in with an alarmingly cheery tone. 'See yirsels out! Nice ti meet yi, hen. See yi later, son. Mind an lock the door.'

She banged the door with a clatter, her steps disappearing down, another clatter and nothing.

Maura smiled at James. He shrugged his shoulders. She shifted her glance to the floor, let it all wash over her. She looked at James again, who laughed.

'That's ma ma then. We'd better get squared up and go, eh?'

When they'd locked the door and were heading down the outside concrete steps, James sighed. 'That wis hell.'

'I thought it was fine,' said Maura. 'I mean, she is just a little bit mad, but better than what I thought she'd be.'

James laughed. 'She always loses the plot like that when she's on the drink.'

'Why did you let her drink, then?' Maura knew it was a stupid question as soon as she asked it.

James didn't give an answer. 'You should a heard her bad mouthin yi when we first went in.'

'It doesn't ever bother me, what people think, James. And anyway,' said Maura, remembering the first conversation she had with Ellen, 'that was before she really met me.'

They didn't speak again till they got to the bus stop. The rain had stopped and the smell of bleach and smoke was still hanging around them. In the shelter, Maura laid her head on James's shoulder and started coughing. They both laughed.

'What a fuckin nightmare she is wi aw that cleanin. Pure stinkin man.'

'I know. And the special vodka tea.'

'An her daft patter aboot you bein destined fur me.'

They laughed again.

'She's a very odd woman.' Maura looked at James. 'That'll be where you get your strange little ways from.'

James didn't answer, just looked back at her, right into her eyes. He smiled and squeezed her hand.

'I killed that guy,' he whispered.

Maura's heart almost burst from her chest. 'I know.'

The bus came round the corner in the distance. She leaned across, put her hands onto his cheeks, held his face to hers and kissed him. Her lips almost devoured his, like she and he were one person.

'That's who we really are, you and me,' she said.

On the bus, Maura drifted back to the first time she saw James, in among the lunchtimers, at the side of the river in the first chill of the autumn sun. He'd been wearing a neat blue zipped jacket with a mod target in the left lapel, and he eyed people up the same way she did. She knew there was something about him, just the way he smiled and held his head.

Three days later, she'd seen him again. She was working in the art store, tidying up the paints, sorting the colours into their schemes and hues in the wooden racks. They were always untidy; as soon as one person looked for a colour, every other one was moved, falling out of rank. James was at the card section, standing back from the rows of different colours, eyeing them up. His long black coat made him look like a thin scraggy boy. It was too big for him, drowned him in tailoring.

She'd heard other girls talk about the moment they saw the man of their dreams, the boy they would be with, and, until then, she thought them stupid and shallow. But there she was, in the art store, looking at this boy, thinking *that might be him*. Crazy woman.

And now, so quickly it seemed, she was here with James, on the bus, coming back from a visit to his mad mother and him telling her about beating that guy up, killing him. She filled with warmth. The world was sitting round her feet, gathering itself in beside her, with her in charge of it all. They sat on the back seat of the bus in silence, not even holding hands. James at her side, his words ringing through her head: *I killed that guy*. Maura knew that the most important thing in life was to be yourself. James had learned to know this too. Without the ability to know yourself, everything else was nothing.

Past Parkhead, the bus juddered to a halt and James put his hand across her to stop her falling. A young man in a white tee-shirt and herring-bone trousers ran through the doors. Once he had his ticket and the bus shifted off, he stood at the front and shouted.

'Gee's a Yeehaaaa.'

Nobody answered.

'Come on ya cunts yis, gee's a Yeehaaaa!'

He looked at everyone in a drunken blur.

'Fur fuck's sake, I thought that this wiz a good bus, a Glesga bus, gee's a fuckin Yeehaaaa!'

A man spoke up. 'It wiz a good bus till you come on, so sit on yir arse and shut the fuck up wee man.'

The bus laughed.

'Fair play big man, fair play,' the young man said.

He sat down next to a young woman with a baby. 'Sorry missus. Nae offence.'

He sat back, gave a thumbs up to the whole bus and closed his eyes.

James took Maura's hand. 'Whit yi want to do, then?'

She thought for a moment. 'Just go into the city and see what happens, I suppose.'

They get off at the next stop. As they alighted from the bus, she said, 'James, do you not think that people on the East Side are more friendly than people on the West? But more aggressive too?'

'It's the East End, no the East Side,' he replied.

Maura said nothing.

They walked from Glasgow Cross down under the railway bridge in the bustle of early evening traffic. They went to the Green a lot, sometimes into the Winter Garden for heat or to get out of the rain, sometimes sitting by the river watching it drift, kissing in the grass, his hand tentatively touching her, hers tentatively touching him.

As they walked, James told her more about the boy and his mother and the fight with the man. He called him the Big Fucker, always with a spit in his tone. He'd left him there, still as a dead dog. Maura felt a thrill course through her as he spoke, squeezed into him, felt his strength and his anger welling up.

Big drops of rain began to fall again. The city responded with a sigh, umbrellas being shaken from bags, cars blinking orange indicators like sparklers, the smell of dust rising from the pavements.

As they reached the high gates, a girl with long blond hair pressed past them, leaving the Green and running at a sudden sprint through the traffic to the other side of the Saltmarket. Her woodland-fresh soapy smell of her reminded Maura of Boroughbridge.

She was back in the tree with Paul. That is where Maura always went in her thoughts when important things were happening. Like a precursor. Or a warning.

'Maura. You listenin ti me?' James nudged her arm.

'Sorry. I was just thinking about something.'

She told him about what happened when Paul died. She told him everything. James listened the whole time without a word as they walked along the crumbling tree-lined paths. The joggers and dog walkers and huddled couples seemed like ghosts to her as she talked. The rain drifted to soft drizzle. The sky darkened as they walked towards the People's Palace and around the football pitches and on down to the river edge. At the car park, they stopped under a tree and looked down into the water and over to the high flats in the Gorbals that were beginning to light up as the day seeped away.

When she'd seen that Paul was dead, Maura had gone back home, leaving him in among the trees and the creatures and the soft wind. There were tears and disbelief.

When the flurry of police and ambulance and rushing to the woods and questions and wailing were over, there were tears again and the slow sorry sinking in.

Her mum diminished, squeezed into a smaller space, un-done.

Her dad, once ebullient and huge, idled onto his couch and hugged anyone who would sit with him.

Maura and James walked back along the river bank and sat on a bench, watching the sky get darker and letting the rain smooth their heads. The wind played with the early leaves on the trees. Children's voices could be heard across the river and occasional shouting. Every so often, footsteps crunched the path behind them.

'Why don't we go to the Star Club the night?' said James.

The Star Club was on the south side of the river, a Communist club that had a rock night that James was always trying to get her to go to.

'It'll be brilliant. Yi'll love it, honest.'

Maura agreed, reluctant at first. She hadn't been out much in Glasgow and standing in a sweaty hall listening to some rubbish music wasn't her first choice. But she felt in her bones that James was nearer to her now, and that she was nearer to him.

'That'll be great,' she said, and squeezed into him again.

There was already a band on the stage when they arrived at the entrance of the Star Club. From behind its diminished Georgian fineness, Maura could hear the beat, and the corridor down towards the music was filled with all ages of people chatting and laughing and drinking. It was £1.10 each to get in. The woman at the small ticket desk had dyed red hair and a hand that only had a thumb and one finger, the rest of them tiny stumps. She gave them their tickets and a flier for an anti-nuclear protest rally the following weekend.

The carpet in the hallway was tatty, with ornate red squares and the hint of a Paisley pattern about it. Every six or seven steps, the curled-up line of a tear was held down by a strip of thick black tape. James tripped on one, stumbled against a tall woman with bright dyed blonde hair.

'Watch where yir fuckin goin ya dick,' she said and turned away, laughing. Her friend, a tall, red-haired boy with a camera round his neck, laughed too.

James stopped, his head down for a second. 'Sorry about that,' he said and looked at Maura. Smiled. When he did that, smiled at her, she felt excited.

The red-haired guy mumbled 'No bother,' and eased himself past Maura and into the main hall.

The woman snarled after him, something Maura didn't catch. Her ear for Glaswegian was well-trained, but the drunker people were, the harder she found it to understand.

The music was pounding and the door into the hall swung back and forth with people leaving and entering. The noise of the band pulsed as the door opened and closed. That smile of James's was like a wash of the tide over Maura, and the music like the warm wind.

The band on stage was playing a cover version of *Like a Hurricane*. Maura took James's hand and whispered 'I love you.'

He looked straight back and said it too.

The air smelt of a strong mix of sweat and spilt beer and cannabis. They found a spot and watched as the lead guitarist raged the screaming guitar solo that lifted the song to its finale. His head stayed down the whole time, his long fair hair dancing back and forth to the music. The singer had black shaggy hair and wore a Rezillos tee-shirt and he rarely took his eyes off the ceiling. Maura had seen the Rezillos' last gig at the Apollo in the first year she came to Glasgow. Fay Fife's mad stamping singing and the pent-up energy of the whole thing.

When *Like a Hurricane* finally ended in a blaze of guitar feedback and drums, the bass player stepped forward. He wore a jacket that was far too big for him and tight stretched denims. When he came out of the light, his blue shirt shone eye-bright on the stage.

'Right thanks, eh, that's eh *Hurricane*, eh. Fuck Trident right!'

A bit of a cheer from the crowd.

'Eh, this wan's *The Vast*. Take it away big man.' He nodded to the drummer who counted them in to a poppy, ringing song that immediately had the crowd at the front dancing.

'That's quite good that wan,' shouted James into Maura's ear. She smiled and nodded back to him, tapping her foot and swinging a bit in time.

'Want a drink?' she shouted to him as the song entered a key change after the middle eight.

'Aye, great, pint a Tennent's then.'

Fighting her way back from the bar, Maura saw James talking to two guys and a girl. The bigger guy had Elvis swept-back hair; the girl had wild straw hair and wore a long floral frock. They kept looking away from James to the band and laughing things to each other. The red-haired guy was there too, his camera up to his eye, snapping the band and various people in the crowd. Beside them, concentrating on the music, a smaller guy drank a can of Coke. He wore round glasses and a black tee-shirt with a skull and crossbones on it.

When Maura handed James his drink, he said to them 'This is ma girlfriend.'

She liked that. She handed him the pint and stroked the side of his face with the back of her hand.

The guy with the camera held his hand up. 'Sorry about that out there, by the way. My sister. Can be a bit of a cow sometimes.'

'No bother, mate,' said James.

Maura said nothing, felt the heat rise in her belly.

'Cheers,' said the guy, and immediately manoeuvred himself round behind Maura and James. 'I'm pals with the *The Promise* up there. I'll get one of you with them in the background. You might see this in a book when they get their deal.'.

Maura smiled and held James close to her.

They stood watching the band for two more songs, then weaved their way to the back of the room. James asked Maura if she wanted another drink, but she didn't. She thought it might be time to take things forward with him. She didn't think it, she knew it. And it wasn't only the warmth in her belly that told her or the tingle in her thighs. Nor only the flush she'd felt run through her when she held his hand as they leaned against the back wall.

'Do you want to go?' she asked him.

He looked up at the band and back at his nearly finished pint. 'Aye. I've heard enough.'

He drained the lager and Maura swallowed the last of her vodka and lime. She didn't feel like drinking too much tonight. Wanted to be at her best.

Outside, the air was cold and it was still raining. It wasn't heavy, but the soft stuff that James called lazy rain because it went through you rather than round you. It settled into greyness and she knew that this was a night that people would want to get home with the least hassle possible. Some nights, even when it rained, people seemed to be up for the town no matter what. Heavy rain could be exciting and invigorating and it made the city dance and pulse. As if Glasgow was built for it. But this kind of rain made people want to be inside. Safe and warm. All tucked up.

'Once yir wet, yir wet,' said James.

Once over the bridge, they walked along the north side of the Clyde, giving a nod to La Passionara as they passed. They walked up Robertson Street past derelict warehouses with buddleia-sprouting windows. At Argyle Street, they swung round and headed up by the grimy bulk of Central Station and into the shelter of its taxi rank veranda.

From their darkened corner, they watched girls crying on each other's arms, an array of vomiting and the occasional mild skirmish as the taxi queue disappeared into black cabs and out into the night.

After a while, Maura tugged James's arm and they went back out into the huddling rain and up to through Royal Exchange Square. At the art store that Maura worked in, they stood looking through the window, arms linked.

'What the heck are we just standing here like this for?' said Maura.

James laughed back. 'I huvnae a fuckin clue.'

Maura reached up and kissed him. They kissed for a few minutes in the doorway of the store, oblivious to the traffic rolling past and the people and the noise and the smell of the city. Everything else was blurred into nothingness.

They walked on, their fingers woven together, past the university and the old buildings of the Merchant City that were beginning to be renovated. Scaffolding and boarded walkways made Maura feel that this might be a good place to hide and wait, but she didn't say this to James who seemed lost in his thoughts, every few moments squeezing Maura's hand or smiling down at her. They reached the High Street, a shabby, undone place that she had been told was where Glasgow started, where the Molendinar Burn still ran in a culvert under the roadway.

'Mon we'll go back ti the Green and see whit we get ti do there, eh?'

Maura didn't have to ask what James meant, just knew. Just felt it.

They headed down past the Tollbooth again, down the Saltmarket with its smells of bus diesel and vinegared chips and once again into the shadows of Glasgow Green.

They sat on a bench among some newly planted rowan trees, snuggling together.

'I think it's time,' said James.

'Time for what?' Maura felt a bit bad saying this, because it was obvious and it was what she wanted almost more than anything. But she needed to hear him say it, to be sure.

James stood up and looked into her face intently, his hands raised like an American television evangelist. He opened his eyes wide, gave a pretend blood curdling laugh, then said in an ominous tone 'Time...' he bent down to Maura and whispered, 'for a killing.'

Maura's stomach tightened and her heart began to race. 'I thought you would never ask, lover boy.'

He kissed her. 'And yi never know what might happen then.'

He sounded like a different person, as if the last few days had unlocked him from a dark prison and he'd eased his way out, not sure of what he would find. Now he was ready, and she would be there with him and he would be with her. It fitted.

'I really love you James.'

'I love you too.'

They left the bench and crossed out of the Green and over the old suspension bridge, eyes now peeled, and into the back end of the Gorbals. Without talking, they wandered down to the riverside, nearly outside the Star Club again, in the now pouring rain, just as a group of people spilled into the street, shouting and dancing and drunk.

Maura recognised the tall Elvis guy and the girl he was with. The skull and crossbones guy and two of their friends from the band were with them too. They headed in the opposite direction with rest of the crowd. Maura and James remained out of sight, in beside a tree on the high end of the river bank, a willow, with trailing branches and the start of green buds.

After about five minutes another group emerged, among them the red-haired guy with the camera. He stood apart from the rest, looking first towards them and then in the other direction, several times, craning his neck.

'Lookin fur his pals,' said James.

'We could be his pals,' said Maura.

'Mhmhmh.' James sniggered. 'That's a good yin ... we could be his pals.'

The red-haired guy started towards them, looking back every few steps, staggering a bit, his camera swinging in front of him, the strap around his neck.

'What'll we do?' said James.

'Go with the flow, I suppose.'

Maura felt clear, no doubts, no fears. This was the right

thing. She stepped out onto the pavement in front of the red-haired guy.

'Hi,' she said.

'Aw, right, it's yous.' He squinted at her, nodding his head to James as he appeared into the dim light. 'Seen ma mates, then?'

'No, sorry.'

Suddenly, James darted forward, grabbed him round the neck, dragged him into the shade of the tree, one hand over his mouth, working hard to get him down onto the ground. Maura went for his knees, pulled them away from his body, felt the hard bones of his legs against her shoulder as she wrapped herself around him and sent the three of them sliding down towards the water. The weight of him and James and her and the wet earth, the smell of beer and rain mixed into the cool spring night. The red-haired guy struggled free, trying to punch and slap his way back up the slope. Maura lunged at him, tumbling them both back down again, the camera, still hanging from his neck, clattered the side of her face. Between them, she and James got him onto his back, one of Maura's hands over his mouth, one of his arms now pinned under her knees. He managed only muffled shouts as he writhed to get away. James knelt onto his legs, finally grabbed his other arm and Maura took that too and knelt on it. She was strong because of the metal work and people were always surprised at that. She put both hands over the guy's mouth and nose and pressed. James took the camera strap and tightened it around his neck. Maura could feel her heart pounding in time to the bucking and muffled squeals and she squeezed with all her strength. The harder she forced down, the closer her face was to James, and she found their lips touching, the guy still writhing under them. A rush through her body as she pushed her lips to

James's, and his hand now between her legs, pressing her and kissing her harder, and the rush and the rain, and the red-haired guy's body thrusting and heart pounding and his breath suddenly choked against Maura's hands.

And still.

James's head buried into her neck, the wet of his hair on her face. The after-rush.

Hard breathing.

Then voices.

On the street.

She tensed, James too. The red-haired guy lay still, nothing. She smiled at James. He winked back at her. Sniggered, his hand up to his mouth to stop the laugh.

Voices, closer.

'Where the fuck did he go?'

'He's a total wank, fuck's sake man.'

Maura's heart beat high and hard in her chest. She shivered. Wiped the rain from her face.

'He'll be up the road, fuck.'

'Aye, mon.'

The red-haired guy didn't move. Maura's breath settled. She looked over to James. He smiled his big wide smile. Her heart slowed.

James tugged the camera from around the guy's neck and laid it to the side.

'I suppose he should go fur a wee swim, eh?'

Maura smiled. 'Okay then, let's do it.'

They hunkered up, James at the feet and Maura at the head, and dragged him to the flat edge of the bank. 'Y'awright?' James whispered. She nodded, and they pushed. The body acquiesced and slid with an almost delicate splash into the water. It bubbled and bobbed for a second, then floated just under the surface and away with the run of the river and into the dark.

Maura caught a brief last sight of his shape as the body disappeared. She wondered if his friends were crossing the bridge at the same time as he floated under it.

She turned to James. He laughed again.

'I think I've definitely given up on bein a good guy.'

'Give me a kiss then,' she said.

III: Maura, girl

*An encounter. – Lessons about sex. – An old woman is
followed. – A resurrection of sorts. – Some things are best
not known.*

MAURA KNELT ON THE LEAF MOULD floor of
the wood and crept gently towards the noise. She
peeked her head over the edge of the mossy rise, careful not to disturb whoever it was. There, on a red tartan
blanket, in the flat grass in the dell, a bare white bum rid-
ing up and down and legs and arms and two heads and
moaning and *cooing* and *oooohing* louder and faster and
slower and quieter and louder and faster again.

Maura pulled her head back into the safety of the shade
of the large plane tree. She didn't know whether to laugh
or be sick. The bluebells swam around her; they rose and
fell on the mottled earth, the sun spangling the floor and
the tree boles. She didn't like other people being there in
the woods. And certainly not if they were doing sex.

The wind breezed, filtering through the leaves, like the
fingers of deaf people talking, fluttering.

Every time Maura stopped at the high plane, she
thought about Paul, every time for the three years it was
since he died. She wasn't sad, of course, but she always
remembered. His laugh and his eyes and the way he
made everything lighter. Her mum and dad had visited
one time only: laid the big stone that her dad had carved
a cross into, not a gravestone, but a boulder he'd found
at the edge of a field on the other side of the brook. The
woods had taken it over now and it was half sunk into the
earth and grown over with mosses.

The noise lifted again from below. Maura's heart *paddum paddummed* in her chest. She snuck her head over to look. She would be unseen and unheard because these were her woods and she knew them like nobody else. The couple were still moving, the white bum bouncing up and down, flashing in the dappled light. Underneath, a woman's hair, black on the red tartan of the rug.

Maura pushed herself closer into the side of the tree, brushing her hand against Paul's stone. She traced around the shape of the cross, the hard stone nuzzling her fingertips. She stood up, holding onto the trunk, ready to dart behind it if need be. She peered as much as she dared down to where the couple were. The woman was Mrs. Spencer who lived in the High Street, just where her gramps was. And the man looked like Mr. Spencer, with his thin body and blonde hair. She noticed that he had a bald patch on the top of his head.

She was glad she hadn't seen Mrs. Spencer with another man. She remembered the trouble at the party with John Wilkes and her Aunt Joanne. Joanne was deaf and Maura associated sign language with excruciating awkwardness from then on. Something she couldn't control. She didn't like not being in control. But she did like the feeling in her stomach at the time.

It was one of the big parties her mum and dad used to have. Before Paul died. Everyone was there: Joanne was up from Birmingham, and all the neighbours that usually hung around were there. Her Nan was still alive and she was there too. Gramps never came to the parties.

In the brimming, *beat beat beat*, Maura sat in the corner of the living room, a good place to get a view of everything. Paul dotted from room to room talking to people, but she didn't do that. Just watched. Joanne was drunk and had fallen asleep on a bench in the garden. When she woke, she staggered back into the house and told everyone she was going to bed, so drunk that her signing was floppy. John Wilkes was there with his wife Uzma and his son Danish. Maura saw Joanne's eyes and John Wilkes' eyes meet. Later, when his wife and their son were ready to go, John Wilkes hung back and Maura knew that he and Joanne had something planned. So when John Wilkes' wife came back half an hour after that asking was he still there, and everyone said he'd gone, Maura had piped up, 'He's up the stairs with my Aunt Joanne,' and the room went quiet, and John Wilkes' wife stomped up the stairs, followed by Maura's mum.

In a minute, there was shouting and yelling and John Wilkes came running down and out of the front door with his shirt in his hand and no shoes on, and his wife running back down in tiny steps, in tears and out the door. Maura's mum came down a bit later, quiet and shaking her head. Her dad changed the music to something loud and rhythmic and he and Maura's mum danced together with their hands flying in the air and they were whispering to each other and laughing and looking up the stairs to where Joanne was and shaking their heads.

Maura loved those parties. And so did Paul. They watched the adults laughing and dancing and drinking in the house and going out to the garden to smoke because her mum and dad didn't allow smoking in the house, even then. Everyone seemed to smoke. And they all shared their cigarettes. Maura liked that, all the adults sharing and laughing and having a good time.

Even better, she knew now that under all that good time was a bad time brewing. And that made her even happier for some reason.

Mr. and Mrs. Spencer *cooed* and *ooohed*, and Mr. Spencer's white bum rose and fell in time to their song. Maura snuggled down into the hollow at the top of the rise and watched. She had to squint her eyes tight to get a proper view, knowing that if she went any closer, she might be heard or seen, and that would be that.

She wondered if she was meant to feel something when she saw sex, a thrill, but she didn't. She sometimes watched the bull in the field between the edge of Boroughbridge and the woods when it was put in with the cows in winter. She watched, fascinated but not excited. Same with dogs in the street, the bitch trying to walk away while the dog scuffled madly at her, his front legs holding on while his back end pumped away at a hundred miles an hour. It was just like that with Mr. and Mrs. Spencer: she watched them on their red checked blanket, his white bum and her wrap-around legs, and their moaning and sighing. They looked as if they belonged in among the trees, with flies buzzing at them and birds singing and chirping as if they were joining in. And their kissing.

Her dad and her mum used to kiss a lot, but less and less now. He sat big and half-dead on the couch and she buzzed around the house, tight and fast and never settling to anything. All since Paul's accident.

A sudden rise of anger. Maura stood up to get a better view. Mr. and Mrs. Spencer were still writhing and moaning on the blanket. Maura went back down the slope, out of sight now, and began to pick up clods of mossy earth and sticks. She piled them on the top of the rise and held her breath. She knelt, firming her knees into the ground to make sure she'd good purchase, and poked her head over the top. She was sure she could hit them without really being seen. She knew they'd want to be seen less than her. She threw the first clod. The stones in it made it heavy enough to be aimed easily, and would give a good hard clout if it hit the target. She missed, but the noise startled them and they stopped. She looked over again. They were hushed and completely still, Mrs. Spencer's legs still raised into the air, but not moving now.

Maura picked up three more clods of earth and threw them one after the other in quick succession. She knew that at least two of them hit because she heard Mr. Spencer shouting 'Bloody hell!' and Mrs. Spencer squeaking. She picked up four sticks in her right hand and let them fly with her left, her good aiming hand. She gathered four more and dared her head over the top of the rise. Mr. and Mrs. Spencer were scurrying to put their clothes on, looking out for more attacks and gathering up the blanket, at the same time. They said 'Bloody hell!' and 'Hurry up!' and 'Who is it?' and Maura, not caring any more about being recognised, rained down sticks and mucky clods of earth and moss on to them. Her aim was good. When Mrs. Spencer was on one foot trying to get into her pants, she took a stick to the side of her face and lost her balance. She fell over and knocked into Mr. Spencer, both of them falling onto the grass. While they were stumbling back to their feet, Maura got them with a mossy clod each, him in the face and her in the bum. She was laughing and throwing and they were desperately trying to get everything together and on and to get away. Mr. Spencer managed to get dressed first and stood in front of his wife, seeking their attacker out. He fixed his eyes on her, shouted 'You boy!' not seeing her hair held back in an elastic band under her skip cap. She hit him in the face with a clod of moss before he followed his wife, who by this time had the blanket in her arms and was running down into the undergrowth towards the brook. They disappeared into the greenness.

She sat back down. Looked round. Her woods. She felt better now that they were gone. Quiet and calm. She lay down, looked up into the canopy of the trees, the light of the sky eking its way through the leaves, the flutter of them twinkling the light in, a *drip drip drip* of light. She closed her eyes. Her heart was still beating strong. The birds settled around the woods and began to sing again. The hum of flies. The soft whisper of the wind playing with the leaves. Her own breath. Her heart loudest of all in her ears.

At school that week, they'd had the Big Girl Talk. She didn't know many of the other kids at that time; they'd only come together in the last three weeks to high school from all around Boroughbridge. From her school, there were her and six others.

'Maura Weightman, would you hurry up.' An angered call from a teacher whose name she didn't know.

She was a tall woman, with a straggle of greying hair and a nose that was too stubbed for her thin face, like she'd swapped her nose with a chubby person. Maura decided immediately that she would like her. 'Sorry Miss, just coming,' and she smiled her one of her really engaging smiles, holding the teeth and eyes for a split second more than usual.

'Good. Thank you, Maura'.

'Now, girls, I do not, repeat not, want you to be silly in the lesson today. The boys have gone with Mr. Tompkins to the gym hall and no doubt they will act immaturely and snigger, but I do not...' she looked round the room at all the faces 'want that from you. Okay?'

Nods. Shuffles. They all knew what was coming. One girl did snigger, but only for a moment till the teacher said, 'Yes? Catherine Auld? Got a problem?'

'No Miss.'

'Good. Let's get started then, shall we.'

Maura looked over at Catherine Auld. Her face was red. Not embarrassed red, but blotchy red, and she wore a pink band in her straw hair that matched the colour of her face.

She sat with her head down when the teacher spoke to her, 'Sorry Miss Trotter,' and smirked to herself and reddened a bit more.

Maura stored Miss Trotter's name at the front of her mind.

She decided would not like Catherine Auld. But she'd probably just leave her alone, *out in the cold*, as her Nan said.

Miss Trotter asked all the girls in the class to put their hands up if they'd started their periods, 'Your monthlies, girls, if you don't know what I mean,' and counted nearly half the class. Maura saw Catherine Auld put her hand up and thought she must be lying, just the way she raised it, kind of half slow and uncertain.

Maura kept her hand down.

'Tell them nothing,' her dad would say. 'Fascists the lot of them.' Her dad was never wrong about things.

Her mum would smile at Maura and rub her dad's head. 'That's enough Tom, you'll have that lass's head as full of rubbish as your own.'

Miss Trotter continued '... and if you look at the way the eggs are stacked up, girls, ready to be launched, one a month, for thirty years or so...' Miss Trotter had drawn a diagram on the blackboard, a shape like a sheep skull with lines leading from it to *womb* and *egg tubes* and *vagina*. But she hadn't drawn the clitoris. Maura wanted to put her hand up and ask why, but she knew that would make Miss Trotter mad so she drifted out of the class again, into a daydream about David Essex. She didn't need to listen to any of this stuff anyway; her mum had told her everything she needed to know and even her dad would answer any questions she had. So she was all right. When she'd been exploring her parents' room one time, she found a book under her mum's pillow called *The Joy of Sex*. Maura had taken to going to her parents' room and reading it. She just knew that Miss Trotter wouldn't be telling them any of the stuff in there.

Maura was aware of a hand going up in the row in front of her. Ann Jenkins, her best friend from primary, was asking 'How does the seed from the man get to the egg Miss, I mean I think I know,' Maura nudged her in the back, 'but I'm not sure.'

Maura knew that Ann Jenkins did know. Maura had told her, but she was always doubtful of the things Maura said, even though she never ever told a lie.

'Well,' Miss Trotter hesitated, 'the man and the woman are in bed together and…connect. They connect. And the seed from the man, the sperm, finds the egg.' She coughed. 'When they connect.'

Maura nudged Ann Jenkins in the back again and she turned round, tight-lipped, stared her best *stop it!* stare and turned back, her shoulders trying hard to stay still as she resisted laughter.

Later, when the boys joined the group again and the class was full, the word went round that James Lazarius had fainted during the Big Boy Talk. Fallen off the table. Everyone in the class looked at him, his face red as word spread. But James Lazarius was a cool boy and pretended to faint again, flipping off his chair. Everyone laughed more and Miss Trotter shouted again. And it all stopped. Like so much of life in school, it all stopped.

Maura thought about Mr. and Mrs. Spencer trying to get dressed and see who she was at the same time. She'd got them a few good ones before they ran away. It made her happy seeing other people sad and upset. Most of the time anyway. Not always. Even when people looked happy, she could see under the smile that anyone offered to what was really there. Not that she was miserable, but she knew that misery was never too far from the surface. Paul thought she was miserable. When he was alive, he would go on and on about it.

They were in their big plane tree and the leaves were only early, and they could see beyond the Devil's Arrows and across the whole flat land around Boroughbridge. Paul pointed his finger and drew it across the arc of the horizon.

'Whooo Maura. Look how far you can see today. Now that is something!'

'Too flat for me. I want to live in the mountains when I grow up. This is boring and flat and too squared off.'

'You're a real misery guts sometimes.'

'And you're a pain in the neck.'

'No, Maura, I mean it. You should try to be more cheery or something.'

Her big brother looked at her right in the eyes, as if he was trying to see what it was. She knew. But she'd hidden it. Deep down. Even then. Even when she was just nine and they were all happy and her dad was joyous and boisterous and her mum was enlivened and creative and sunny. And Paul was alive. Even then, before it all slipped, Maura had something hidden away deep down. Only when she was on her own did she really let it out, and no matter how much Paul wanted to find it, he never would. Because it was hers. It was the seed that she was nurturing, in all that good, joyous, happy soil in her family. She didn't know what it was then, but she knew she needed it. She knew she needed to keep it secret too, so what she let creep out was *misery guts*.

Paul looked at her for a short time, then

'Misery guts!'

'Pain!'

'Misery guts!'

'Pain!'

'Misery guts!'

'Pain!'

'Misery guts!'

'Pain!'

She pushed him, and he pushed her, and they scrambled like monkeys down the tree and shouted as they launched from the lower branches onto the dark woodland floor,

'Misery guts!'

'Pain!'

'Misery guts!'

'Pain!'

'Misery guts!'

'Pain!'

They laughed and pushed each other again, down into the wood sorrel and ferns and the smell of wild garlic and the squawk of birds' alarm calls. They ran after each other, brother and sister, happy and shining

'Misery guts!'

'Pain!'

'Misery guts!'

'Pain!'

Into the dark wonderful wood.

Maura lay on the leafmeal floor of the wood, the sun

and the cool breeze beating like a soft heart around her. The early leaves of the trees cast everything green and peaceful, even the birds had quietened down once Mr. and Mrs. Spencer left. When she opened her eyes, she stretched herself awake and crawled back over to the base of the big plane. She sat down beside Paul's stone again. She cleared the moss away from the grooves her dad had made for the cross and scraped back the grass. She stood up and smiled. The stone sat now in a rough circle of bare earth, settled. She walked round it, looked up into the tree.

Paul's face beamed a smile at Maura as he reached back into the green leaves for the next hold to climb higher. She was near the bough, he towards the middle of the branch. It was their tree and the trunk was scarred with their initials that they'd scraped and edged with knives over the years. He should have been able to easily find a friendly branch, but he didn't. Maura watched as his eyes shifted from smilingly blue to narrowed and afraid and she saw him slide backwards from the branch, heard him gulp a muffled something, and disappear into the green, drowning in the foliage. He thudded several times against the tree before he hit the leaf-moulded earth below. A softer sound than when he had hit the branches.

Silence. She looked down into the green leaves, listening as the birds began their songs again and the insects began to hum again and the wind picked its way through the leaves again. As if all were well.

She climbed ever so carefully to the floor of the wood, eased her feet and hands onto the well-worn holds, and landed soft and safely at Paul's feet. She looked down at him. His body lay stretched out, his feet towards the tree, one straight, the other twisted round as if it were put on backwards. One hand was under him and the other lay outstretched. He didn't move at first, but when she bent down to look into his face, she saw a quick breath lift his chin and a tiny flame light his half-opened eyes.

She walked round him, stepping over his feet, one at a time, and round, over his outstretched hand, and nudged the back of his head lightly with the side of her foot as she passed. A breeze sang high above her.

She kneeled down, facing him. Again, a tiny light, but so small a breath that if it was there at all she couldn't detect it. She wasn't afraid. Her dad and mum had told her to never be afraid, to look at every bad thing as a thing to be overcome.

But a small fear did worm into her head and, as the tiny light flickered, the fear grew: that she would be left with this, a crippled brother.

Not a friend or a brother at all really.

She waited there, kneeling again and looking into his face.

Then the light faded, doused in the cool shade of the tree, and she knew she need have no more fear. She left him there and walked home.

Maura touched the top of Paul's stone, then looked up into the green of the tree. She reached up onto the lowest branch and swung herself against the trunk. She used the purchase to scramble on top of the branch and paused. As soon as she was in a tree, she felt free. As if everything was left behind on the floor of the wood. She swung herself round to face the trunk, then clambered and shuffled, eased her way up and up. She came to the spot she shared with Paul, the spot he'd fallen from three years before. On the bark were their carved initials. Paul was always trying to get her to stop doing it.

'It'll ruin the tree, Maura. They're creatures like you and me.'

She sat back and breathed the soft air, closed her eyes. The breeze whispered through the leaves.

The top of the tallest of the Devil's Arrows peeked above the trees in front of the town. The sharp tip rose like a finger pointing to the sky. Her dad said that spacemen had put them there so they knew where to land their spaceship. Even Maura knew he was talking rubbish that time. She loved them, giant slabs of stone thrusting out of the ground. Sometimes she went to visit them early in the morning, before anyone else was up, and walked in among the three huge standing stones. She always felt happy when she went back home for breakfast then.

In the distance, a grey cloud was beginning to puff up. It might rain tonight, she thought.

She clambered back down and jumped from the lowest branch, landing softly. The sun sliced through the trees, but the wind rose a bit and bent the grass and the leaves back and forth.

The woods led out into a field with a walkway alongside an old stone wall. She followed this until she saw two people ahead of her. She recognised Mrs. Ripon, who stayed at number six down the road from her house, and her grandson, a blonde frail-looking boy a few years younger than Maura. They were heading back to the main road into town. Maura decided to follow them. She adjusted her skip cap to shield the sun from her eyes and walked after them, keeping her distance.

The boy's blonde hair flopped when he walked, side to side like a girl's. Mrs. Ripon walked slowly, using her stick on the rougher parts of the path.

Maura often followed people. She imagined doing bad

things to them sometimes, but she never did, just got good at following without being caught.

When they got to the town, Mrs. Ripon went into the baker's shop at the bottom of High Street. The blonde boy stayed outside and kicked the wall till his grandmother came back out and told him to stop it. She handed him a bag with cakes or pasties or something in it. Probably going to the park for a picnic, thought Maura. But they didn't. They turned onto York Road and waited at the first bus stop, the boy looking into the bag and smiling up at his grandmother, who shook her head and rubbed his hair. She said something to him that Maura couldn't hear and they both smiled at each other. Happy.

Maura left them to their stupid happiness and headed home. As she turned the corner into her street, Mr. and Mrs. Spencer were driving down towards her in their car. Maura wondered where they'd been all this time; perhaps panicking somewhere, wondering if everybody in Boroughbridge would know what they'd been doing. It wasn't Maura's style. She kept secrets really well.

Maura had already unbound her hair from its elastic band, but there was still a threat of possible recognition: she decided not to care. She stopped at the junction just as the car arrived. Mrs. Spencer was nearest her in the passenger seat and had a graze on the side of her face. Her hair was dishevelled. Mr. Spencer's head was smeared with mud and his shirt was dirty. As he looked up and down the street each way, Maura saw that Mrs. Spencer was laughing. She leaned in close to Mr. Spencer, said something to him, and he laughed too. The car wound round the corner with both of them laughing. Maura followed them with her eyes, watched till the car disappeared over the brow of the hill. She crossed over and headed home.

It was then she saw them. Her mum and dad on the pavement along from the house.

Her dad had sat on his couch in their lounge for three years and never got up. Only to go to the toilet or to go to bed or sometimes, when the notion was on him, to have a shower. He never left the house. Every day since Paul's accident, Maura came in from school, or from playing, or from walking in her woods and sat in beside him, snuggled in neatly between his great bulk and the worn arm of the couch. 'I love you Dad'. He'd look into her eyes and say, 'I love you too'. She did love him. Even from the half-deadness of his couch, he made her feel good.

He was always fat, ever since she could remember. He would stand in the hall of their house, laughing and swaying his big belly, uncovered to the vest, and order them: 'Run into my belly'. She and Paul would laugh and squeal 'No Daddy please, not that, anything but that!' and already be scraping the carpet like a bull in a bull fight and Chaaaaaaaaaaaaaarge! head down straight into the soft mass of him. First one, then the other, and if either of them had a friend visiting, they'd be ordered too, and no matter how hesitant, or shy or whatever, they'd end up running and laughing, falling full tilt into the great belly. But not since Paul's accident.

When Maura saw him there, walking on the pavement in front of the house, her mum on his arm, she stopped and stared. His legs were large and unsteady, his gait faltered. He was slow and lumbering and he held a stick like the one Moses had. His long hair was held back in a ponytail and his dark blue pyjama bottoms twisted round his legs. His beige anorak sat unhappily over his broad shoulders. Her mum stepped with him, a tiny ant holding him up.

When her mum and dad saw her, they stopped too. All

three stood motionless in the street, like a Wild West gun fight halted in mid draw. Everything in the street blurred as Maura looked at her dad and then her mum and then her dad again. Her mum's face was drawn and tight, more than usual, and a black smudge of mascara shaded her eyes. Her dad smiled at Maura, held her gaze for a moment, then looked down to her mum and squeezed her closer into him. They turned together and headed back to the house.

There was a smell in the air like when her mum had just opened a window to let the outside come into the house. The same sudden chill had come from somewhere, swept over the street, into her face, reaching right into the very inside of her. Maura breathed the smell in, the warming air of springtime suddenly clutched back to winter. She stood for a minute until her mum and dad disappeared into the greening garden.

She knew that another misery was visiting. Her dad wouldn't be out in the street smiling at her with that particular smile if there wasn't something wrong.

When she went into the house, they were standing in the middle of the living room, very nearly like one person, each holding the other tight and safe.

'We need to talk to you, pet,' her dad said.

A strange pair of slow dancers.

She sat in front of them on the floor.

They, together in their skirting round the issue.

She, straining to hear through the words to the meaning.

IV: James, boy

In the woods. – Quiet moments in the Chapel. –
Confrontation about hair, then tea and biscuits. –
A family dispute. – A visit to the hospital.

JAMES PROPPED THE MIRROR against the gatepost
and drew the scissors from his sock. He squinted to
get a good look. The mirror was cracked, and a few tri-
angles of glass were missing. His face looked back at him
from different directions. In some bits, it was one eye, or
an ear, but in others he could pretty much see his whole
face if he held his head far enough back. The bruise on
the side of his face had moved from red to purple, yellow-
ing now about the edges.

His ma poured him juice from the jug into the green
plastic beaker. He slurped it and choked, spluttered some
onto the table.

'Fuckssake!' His da banged the table and his ma's hand
sliced across the side of his head. It stung.

She was up and had a cloth in an instant, cleaned the
juice, silent. James looked up at her, but she just kept her
eye on the cloth and the juice, lips pursed.

'Ya fuckin little bastart!'

James looked back to his dinner. Throat too tight to
eat.

He stabbed a carrot with his fork, rubbed it in gravy
and put it into his mouth. Soft. Then a piece of the stew.
He didn't like the feeling in his mouth. Hard to chew. But
the gravy was greasy and tasty. A drop fell from his fork
onto the white surface of the table. He smeared it with
his finger and sucked it.

His da jumped out of the chair, filling the room with rage and squeezed his ma's neck. 'Don't you fuckin start me again ya bitch!'

James put another piece of carrot into his mouth.

His ma screamed. Plates crashed. James held the side of his plate, keeping it steady. He looked up. Watched.

His ma screamed. 'Leave me alone'

'Who the fuck are you talking ti ya bitch,' and he punched her right in the face. She fell over against the table, James's dinner spilling from his plate.

James put his head down and looked at his hair. He took the fifty pence piece out of his pocket and turned it over in his hand. It would definitely be fine.

He knelt down, squinted again to make sure he'd the best view, and made the first cut. He liked the *squeeek* and *snik* of the scissors as they cut through the clumps of hair.

Squeeek.
Snik.
Squeeek.
Snik.
Squeeek.
Snik.

He became more confident and cut faster, shifting his head to get the best reflection. The noise changed.

Squeek-snik.
Squeek-snik.
Squeek-snik.
then
Squinik.
Squinik.
Squinik.

And finally, when he was tidying up the loose bits that had escaped

Squik. Squik. Squik. Squik. Squik.

He was finished in five minutes. He rubbed his hands across his hair. It felt good. He sheathed the scissors back in his sock and stood up. He lifted the mirror, holding it at arm's length, and surveyed the result. He took the money out of his pocket and smiled, before placing it carefully back.

The mirror was one of those big ones from a lorry that must have been knocked off when it hit a tree or another lorry or something. He held the bracket and tilted it back and forward to check his hair. Perfect. Behind the far corner of the courtyard of the derelict kennels, the space between the palings and the hedges narrowed until there was nothing. He threw the mirror high into the air and over the palings into the yard. Sprinkles of glass flew off it when it landed on the concrete.

James looked up at the trees. He always felt his stomach lift when he saw them, high against the sky. Green and dark against the grey sky.

The woods were his. He felt safe there on the half-sunned edges of them, and in the cool shadowed heart of them. They smelt safe.

He picked his way alongside the fence, past nettles and brambles and out into the scraggy square of grass that led to the edge of the woods. He squeezed himself between the bole of an ancient beech and an overgrown hawthorn bush and out into a track that was high with grass in the middle and rutted along the sides. The smell of the beech tree rubbed onto his clothes and face. He liked that smell, as if he were a tree or something.

Stepping onto the track he heard the low moan of an engine. He stopped dead, then reversed into the cover of the beech tree. A blue tractor rumbled past with a steel bucket on the front carrying two dead sheep. The farmer didn't see him. From the dark of the tree, James watched the sheep bounce about inside the bucket as the tractor splashed through the rutted puddles on its big wheels, their heads flopping up and down and their legs like the stiff arms of daleks waving in the air. He stayed in the shade of the beech, unseen, till it passed.

The tractor rounded to the farmhouse that poked its chimney pots above the hill to his right. He headed down in the other direction, his heart beating fast.

When he came to the edge of the wood, he stopped. Even from here, he could hear the diggers. They worked every day, even weekends. Like huge wasps, they buzzed and scraped. The smell of the woods met him, damp and fresh and welcoming. He kicked an empty tin can into the soft grey grass and made his way over to the fence. He pulled the wire down a bit, making sure to have a good grip of the barbs that ran along the top, and eased one leg over, then the other. His foot spludged in the mud on the other side of the fence. He didn't care.

He picked his way through the trees. The soft trails of birch fluttered on his face. His legs caught on the trailing brambles that spread out at knee height, spinning their arms out to grab at his legs and drag him into their very heart.

'What you fuckin gawkin at? Wee fucker.'

All the time snarling at him, snarling and raging.

'Bitch ... I'll fuckin kill yi.' Smack! Right in the face 'bastart!'

A spot of blood on the white table. James looked at it. He wondered if it was his blood or his ma's. He smeared it onto his finger and sucked it. The bitter taste.

James picked up a stick and swashed the brambles. *Hee! Haa!* He Kendoed them like Nagasaki. *Whoyawww! Ha!* It was easy for him. These were his woods.

He stopped for a moment and listened to the noise of the diggers. The nearer he got, the more like a rumble it sounded, and he knew that as soon as he lifted himself over the drystane dyke at the far edge of the wood and scrabbled up that last rise, he'd hear them like bombers in a war film, droning and wasting the land below.

He decided to stay in the trees for a bit. He leaned on his stick and surveyed the dead arms of the brambles he'd fought with. They lay, chopped and dead, on the damp earth, winding among the mosses and wood sorrel. He picked a piece of sorrel and nipped a leaf with his teeth. He felt the bitter taste on his tongue and savoured it for a moment before spitting out the green mash. His da had always told him not to swallow the mash because too much sorrel juice would give him a bad stomach and maybe even kill him. But he was fine. He knew what he was doing.

Whoyawww!

One time James saw a guy doing a jobby in the woods. His big white arse shone in the mottled green of the trees. James thought he might be a bad man, thought he kind of looked at him before he turned his back and pulled his trousers and his pants down and squatted just above the ground. James wouldn't like to do that in case a nettle jagged his arse. But the guy didn't get his arse jagged. Just did a jobby. James felt a bit funny when he saw the jobby coming out. He nearly laughed, but thought the guy might turn round and see him. Then he thought the guy might chase him with a big jobby hanging out of his arse. Then he did laugh and the guy did turn round.

He stopped laughing.

Stayed still.

Tried to hide in the trees.

Be green like the undergrowth.

Like nettles.

He liked not being seen; if he could never be seen again he would be happy.

James stood on top of the broken dyke. There was a swathe of grass and birch in front of him. He climbed up there till he reached the top of the short slope with a whole line of rhododendrons running along the top. The earth under rhododendrons was always bare.

The noise was louder now and the mudscape rolled out in front of him. It was scarred and scraped by the giant machines, monster diggers filing back and forth in their big yellowness with tiny wee ant men in them pulling the levers up and down and across and back, and huge trucks piling over the earth in a madness of scraping and pulling, the soil and rocks shoved into giant piles and mashed into the ground, trees ripped by their roots split like giant ice-lolly sticks, the wee men bobbing their heads back and forward in their cabs. At first James could only see six, then two more diggers raced down a long slope, bobbing up and down as they hit the bottom. There were smaller ones too; some of them had buckets and were scraping or lifting or shifting. Others were pounding the earth with huge prongs.

This is what they did. Men sat in their cabs, back and forward scraping the ground, flattening it and ripping it up, flattening it and ripping it up. All day.

As he watched, he heard voices drift up from the brown and grey sweep of land. He looked down under the slope and saw four men stood round a large piece of paper held down at its edges by stones. Each wore a hard hat, two yellow like the diggers, a red one and a white one. He couldn't hear what they were saying.

Then another boy, younger than him with blonde scraggy hair and wearing a bright blue tee-shirt came running down from somewhere behind him. He slid and stumbled down the slope, skipping over the shrubs and stones. The men looked up as he fell over rocks and splashed though the muddy puddles till he finally reached them. One of the men gesticulated, waving the boy back up, but he kicked his feet against a big rock and shuffled round to another of the group, looking down at the paper on the ground.

The men started their conversation again, looking round every so often in one direction or the other, the wee boy turning his head in every direction they did.

One of the men pulled out sweeties and handed them round, finally offering them to the boy, who took one and handed the packet back. Another took out cigarettes and offered them to two of the other men. The boy looked from one to the other as they lit up. The men went back to the paper and to their pointing and looking.

James began to feel cold and was nearly fed up enough to move on when he heard a noise behind him. When he looked round, a bright yellow figure stumbled through the bracken and the birch trees towards him. He scrambled across the edge of the rise and snuck himself under a fallen tree trunk, a thick woody birch. He gathered some loose branches around him and waited. His heart pumped loudly in his chest and up into his throat.

The figure arrived, puffing and cursing under her breath. It was a woman wearing black trousers and a big yellow shirt. She was fat and red faced and said *fuck* or *fuck off* or *bloody fuckin shite!* every time she slipped or tripped or hit her leg on a stick.

James held his breath. Held his big laugh right back in. The woman didn't see him. His heart was still in his throat, loud and strong. She scrambled to the top of the rise.

James edged forward, staying behind the big trunk, till he could just crane his neck enough to see the woman.

She shouted down into the mudscape

'Raymond!'

'Raymond!'

And in a lower tone

'I'll kill im.'

James stretched his head out of his hiding space enough to see both the woman and the group around the paper. The boy looked up at her. The men looked up too. She shouted again.

'Raymond!'

The boy moved to the back of the men and returned to the job in hand.

'Raymond!'

Her voice higher each time.

'Raymond!' On this occasion, she shrilled to herself. 'I will, I'll fuckin kill im.'

The men round the paper started talking and pointing and looking again.

The woman shifted closer to the edge and looked like she might fall. James hoped she would.

'Raymond! Come up here now and we'll get ice cream after yir tea!'

The boy turned away from the paper and scraped up the hill. The men laughed.

Under her breath, 'I really am goney fuckin kill im this time.'

When he reached the top of the slope, out of breath and covered in mud, the boy panted. 'I'm sorry, Mammy, I really am, can I really get ice cream Mammy?'

His ma reached her hand out to his, and, as soon as she had it, she pulled him towards her. With the other hand, she swung a long springy stick she'd lifted off the ground. It hit the wee boy on the legs, then on the side head, then his back and then his legs again.

'You're getting fuck all ice cream!'

'I'm sorry Mammy I'm sorry,'

The stick kept swinging back and across him and back and across.

The anger rose in James as he watched the stick swing back and forward and the noise of the diggers rumbling and the boy screaming and the men laughing and the woman in the fat shirt swearing and hitting, dragging the wee boy back up into the woods. Like a big yellow spider with a fly.

James felt the scissors press against his calf. He pulled his trouser leg up and slipped the steel points out of his sock.

He knew he could stop her with the scissors. He imagined her reeling back against the tree, as he held tight onto the handle, the steel points sliding out of her skin as she staggered back. Against the tree, down the slope, down into the mudscape and sinking into the rubble and the puddles, her yellow shirt blood-soaked, her legs sticking up into the air like big fat sausages.

After the wee boy and his ma were gone, the occasional 'naww' and 'whaah' span in and out of James's ears. He caught a brief glimpse of yellow through the green, with each fainter squawk, a flash of yellow. He lay on his back on the tree trunk, looked up into the branches, the sound of diggers burring, the screams gone into the outside of the woods, nothing. Above him, a sparrow-hawk darted, angled through the trees. It sat for a moment on a low branch on a spindly ash, then disappeared into the dark of the woods.

His ma got the birch from the garden and thrashed and thrashed and thrashed till weals ...
'I'm sorry Ma. I'm sorry'
She took the stick across his legs sore.
Sore.

James looked down over the mudscape again. The big yellow diggers rumbled on and the men faded into the grey brown expanse across the slope on the other side, their coloured hard hats shining out in the wasteland.

He looked beyond the mudscape to the field that stretched up, flat and smooth. At the top of the field, the steeple of Bartonshill Kirk sliced the sky, pointing to the clouds.

One time James had snuck into the kirk and climbed the spiral stair inside the tower till he came to a platform with four cross-shaped windows. From each he could see a completely different view.

From one, he saw over to Coatbridge and Airdrie and beyond.

Another way, he could see the Lochs, over the birch woods at Heatheryknowe where he would lose himself in the trees, falling waist deep into ditches. He wouldn't be able to do that when they got the motorway built. The Lochs looked like daft wee puddles from up there. Along the canal, a ribbon of trees.

From the third window, fields in the distance till his bit, till the kennels and the Chapel and the Edinburgh Road.

When he squeezed his head into the last window, he could see down over the back end of Bargeddie and the fields where his ma took him for picnics. For miles and miles were hills with bits of towns and farms, all rolling together in the big mat of Lanarkshire. His da always went on about Lanarkshire; how it was God's own country and all about the people and the mining and the farming. James hated Lanarkshire.

He looked back over to where the hard hat men had been; there was no sign of them now. He picked up a stone the size of his fist and tossed it from hand to hand. He lobbed it, underarm, high into the air and watched it soar black into the sky, stop for a half a second and dive down past him again and land shphlutt! in a muddy squelch at the bottom of the slope. It disappeared; he couldn't pick it out from the rest of the grey-brown.

He turned and shouted a *Yee!* and a *Haah!* to a fallen tree trunk and jumped onto the top of it. He ran along the first part of its length, then side-footed till it became too bouncy and he'd to hold on to the higher branches to keep himself steady. He jumped to the ground, careful not to land on a stone, because you could break your ankle and might have to stay in the woods for days if you couldn't walk.

He put his hand across his head. The haircut still felt good. Time to go home.

When he reached the edge of the lane, James squeezed out of the gap between the big beech tree and the palings. The tree rubbed itself onto him again and it roughly stroked his leg through his trousers.

'See yi later, tree,' he said.

The tree just stood, not answering, staring from its huge high branches into the beyond, to all the places you could see from a steeple and more.

When he got to the Edinburgh Road, James stopped before crossing. It had six lanes and was mad full of cars and buses and trucks when it was busy. That was why they were building the new motorway. His da said that it would be like a graveyard on the Edinburgh Road when the motorway opened. James always started off with his eyes closed. Eyes tight shut, step off the pavement. He would check the length of the road both ways first of course. He nearly got hit by a bus one time, and the bus driver had got out and chased him when it had swerved and screeched to a halt.

'Ya daft wee prick!'

Today, the road was quiet. At the traffic lights, a green van was waiting, he knew he'd have time but. He shut his eyes, stepped out and stopped. Listened for the rev of an engine, then carried on over to the central reservation and slipped through the grass. As soon as he set foot onto the other side, a car horn blared and he jumped back. Kept his eyes shut. He smiled. He was in charge today. He wiped his hands on his trousers and made a breenge across the road. When he reached the pavement, he tripped over the kerb, but managed to keep his feet. He breathed in and out for a moment, then opened his eyes.

One of the nuns from the convent was looking at him. About ten feet away. He looked back at her. Her face was framed by the white rim of her veil, her glasses held together by sticky tape. She shook her head at him and walked on, stopping at the edge and looking both ways before crossing, deliberately, to the middle. James flicked two fingers at her and ran down the road.

When he turned into his street, he felt a twist in his stomach. He knew something wasn't right, but he couldn't feel for certain what it was. He had felt this lots of times before. Sometimes when it happened, he felt a rush in between his legs, like a sherbet dip or the feeling a chute gives you.

He stayed on the side with the houses. The trees on the other side seemed to lower themselves at him as he ran past, reaching down to catch him or skite him or sweep him up into the air and land him sore on his arse.

A double-decker bus shuntered past, grinding its gears, hissing its air brakes and swirling and spitting dust at him. As he crossed the road at the Chapel, the rain began to fall. At first, it was just wee drops, then in a second everything darkened and rain spread across the ground, spilling a sweet dusty smell into the air.

He went into the Chapel. His ma and his da brought him here every Sunday. They wanted him to be an altar boy, but he didn't like the idea of being up there with everyone looking at him, or having to get the priest all the things at the right time, sitting in a black frock ringing the bells and getting it wrong and everyone laughing at him or getting him into trouble for being an eejit. There were two priests, Father Lowe and Father Fitzpatrick, and they were nice to James and everybody else, but that didn't mean that he wanted to be an altar boy or anything.

A huge stained-glass window rose on the wall at the far end, the front of the church. The Creation Window. It floated high, and beat like a heart with the sun moving its colours, and sometimes at Mass the incense rose up into the air round about it. In the middle of the window, Jesus smiled down at him, and angels flew, blowing trumpets, and all around the top there were stars and the moon and the sun. His favourite bit was in the bottom half. Fish and birds floated and flew on the outside and a big cow and a lion squatted, facing each other, and Adam and Eve were there. He always thought that Eve looked like a man because her hair was tied back or in a bun or something and she didn't have the shape of a woman. The moon was a black circle of glass that sat out from a ring of white around its edge, so that it always looked like a crescent whatever direction you were looking at it from. Right at the very bottom, coiled and ready, hid a snake.

When the cool air of the Chapel hit him, the jumpiness in his stomach left. He went through the middle doors and stomped down the aisle as loud as he could. His feet slapped the tiles and the noise reverberated high into the ceiling space, echoing off the walls all round him. He was the only person there. When he got to the third row from the front, he stopped, looked up at the Creation Window and tried again to see if he could see tits on Eve.

He squeezed into a seat and slid along till he was nearly at the end of the pew. This was his favourite, where he could be hidden from view behind the massive sandstone pillar. Like the other seven pillars, this one rose high into the roof and held giant arches that spanned all the way across. He rubbed the top of his finger on the rough surface, felt the grains of sand move under his skin. He did this every time he sat in this seat. He sometimes wondered if he could rub the pillar away if he did it long enough. Grains of sand would loosen themselves and lodge on his skin.

He felt the scissors pressing against his leg. He took them out and looked at them. The shiny blades reflected the darkness in the void of ceiling above him. He used the edge to scrape sand from the pillar; a shower of grains fell from the scissors' path as he pushed the blades up. He did it again and more fell. He repeated this seven or eight times, then examined his work; not much difference really. He pressed his finger onto the point of the scissors. The hard metal bit into his flesh. He thought about the wee boy at the mudscape and wished he had

98

stabbed his stupid ma. He imagined her lying there, all blood and muck in her fat yellow dress, and the wee boy crying *Mammy! Mammy! No ma Mammy!* and the men running up from their work to try and save her and there was nothing anyone could do about it because he'd done it right through her heart. That was why there would be so much blood.

He stood up and leaned his weight onto his hands and onto the scissors and against the surface of the pillar. He started to write, shifting the angle of the scissor points until he had finished. When he sat back down, he looked up at the faint *HA HA* he'd scratched onto the stone.

He heard a door opening and closing in the sacristy off to the left; probably one of the priests coming in, or the housekeeper. He took the flat edge of the scissors over the words he'd written. They disappeared easily under a snow storm of sand, leaving only the faintest line of an *H* and cross bar of an *A*. Once he'd finished, he replaced the scissors in his sock, headed up the side aisle, with a glance back to the big cow on the window, and left.

The rain had slowed to a drizzle by the time he got outside again. As he crossed the road to his house, the feeling in his stomach started to come back. He climbed the stairs to the front door and opened it, the sound of his ma's voice rising from the kitchen and the laugh of a visitor in reply.

'That you, son?'

'Aye, Ma.'

'Git yir hair cut?'

'Aye, Ma.'

'Mon in and let me see, then.'

When he entered the kitchen, Mrs. Henry, from next door, was seated at the table with a cup of tea and his ma was peeling spuds at the sink. As she turned to look at him, James saw her face change.

'What's happened to you?'

'What?' he replied, suddenly knowing fine well what, but not able to think what to do about it.

She changed tone. 'D'yi get yir hair cut then?' Softly.

'Aye.'

'Well, mon you wi me back down ti Alex Jordan's an I'll give him a haircut wi ma bare hauns. Huv yi seen,' her voice raised, 'the fuckin state of yi?'

'What?' Indignation now in his voice.

She was round the table at him, had him by the back of the jersey and the ear at the same time and marched him into the front room and up against the mirror.

The hair cut hadn't been a success. One half was short and very nearly neat, but the other was spiky and chewed looking, and his fringe was into the wood on one side of his forehead and almost in his eye on the other. He couldn't see the back, but he knew that it wasn't much better.

'I'll ask yi again. Where'd you get it cut?'

Mrs. Henry, her face holding in a laugh, appeared at the door.

'You dae that yirsel son?'

'Aye.'

James felt his stomach heave and his face burn.

His ma skited the side of his head with the back of her hand. 'Where's the money then?'

He fished in his pocket and brought out the fifty pence.

Mrs. Henry piped up, 'I'm goin doon the street, Ellen. Will I take im wi me and he can git it fixed?'

His ma relinquished her grip. 'That would be nice, thanks.'

James felt his stomach tighten and loosen, tighten and loosen. As Mrs. Henry led him out, his ma caught up with him and whispered in his ear.

'Wait till I tell yir da about this.'

His ma hardly spoke to him that night. And his da hadn't appeared by the time he was already in his bed, his hair sorted by Alex Jordan, the Spangle that all boys got from him well sooked and its last glassy remains crushed between his back teeth to make sure it didn't cut his insides open.

He shifted his legs slowly about the bed, seeking the cooler corners. He listened to his ma in the front room talking on the phone. He couldn't make out what she was saying, but her voice rose and fell like a wind and he caught the swish of her tones, *wissiwis wissiwisah*, again and again like the swirling spell-cast of a thousand witches. It rose in his ears and faded into his stomach again and again as he tried to find sleep. The voice of witch-mammies hissed, and even the warm rim of the blanket tight across his chin didn't comfort him.

The witch-mammies crept to the edge of him, *wissiwis wissiwisah, wissiwis wissiwisah, wissiwis wissiwisah* around and around and deeper down into him. *Wissiwis wissiwisah, wissiwis wissiwisah*, they feared him into the lull of slumber.

He woke in the dark of the night at a sudden stomach-turning bawl from the front room. The sound of something breaking and his da's voice, loud and angry and his ma screaming and his da hitting and shouting and roaring.

'Right, if yi want me ti hit im I'll hit him ya fuckin boot.'

101

'Leave him! Leave him!'

The screaming and shouting and stomping exploded from the front room for a split second, then James's room door burst open. The shadowed silhouette of his da came out of the sudden light and onto him and he was pulled up by the neck and then the slaps and punches on his face and his body, and his ma screaming 'Naww!' and James was feeling everything sore and his da's breath stinking of smoke and drink and saying to him in a quiet voice 'Ya wee bastart I'll fuckin kill yi' and shouting back to his ma 'Are yi happy noo ya cunt, are yi happy noo?'

When he stopped, James crumpled into the blanket's safe arms and his ma was quiet too and James was crying and his da stomped about the room hitting the walls with his big fist and kicked his ma in the head as she sat down at the door frame, a silhouetted kick and he roared a giant 'Aaaarrrrrrrgggghhh!' as he threw himself into the front room and slammed the door behind him.

His ma stood up. She wiped the side of her face and sorted her skirt. She walked across to James's bed.

'You shouldn't ha done that ti yir hair.'

She tucked the blanket back round his chin and left the room, her shadow darkening as she went through the door, pulling it closed behind her.

James lay there in his tears, his legs still shaking. His stomach tightened and loosened and tightened and loosened. Everything was quiet in the front room.

He was asleep in minutes.

James watched over everything from a secret, hidden place, a huge tree that stood at the centre of a field. He felt warm and safe in its high branches.

The swarm of insects swept up over the hill, chasing

the giant. James sat in his branch and watched, knowing nothing could touch him there.

The insects swarmed around the giant, diving and swishing in unison, and the giant couldn't escape.

The giant ran down the hill screaming and, as they got closer, he could hear the giant's voice, growling and snarling.

James still wasn't afraid.

As the giant hurtled towards the base of the tree, the swarm of insects swirled and dived and bit and stung and hissed, first faintly, *wissiwis wissiwisah, wissiwis wissiwisah,* then rising and rising till he could hear the voice of the swarm crushing his brain and the face of his ma on each of the insects *wissiwis wissiwisah, wissiwis wissiwisah, wissiwis wissiwisah.*

The giant fell against the base of the tree and James could feel the whole tree shake, but he held on and held on and held on. As he lay there, the insects swarmed around him and disappeared inside the giant's screaming body.

James woke to the sound of his ma shouting.

'He's at the bottom of the stairs, come quick, there's blood everywhere!'

He jumped out of bed and ran into the bright light of the hall. He heard his ma slam the phone down and she rushed out of the front room past him. The door to the stairs was open and he followed her there. She was standing looking down to the main door of the flat. She didn't speak, just breathed heavily. James's da lying at the bottom.

One of his legs was on the first stair, and the other was under his body, twisted. His head was lying against the closed door, his face staring upwards, eyes open.

'We'll have to move him to let the ambulance in,' his ma said and she motioned to James to follow her down the stairs.

She picked up a bottle half full of vodka from the top landing. She tutted, took out a hanky from her pocket and wiped blood from the bottle and the wall and the banister. She looked hard at James and led him down to where his da was lying.

They could hardly move him. He was wedged at an angle and they could only get near him by standing on the first step. They tried to take an arm each and pull, but that was no good, and every time they moved him an inch his da made a low gargley wheeze.

After a while, there were sirens in the distance mixing in with the grunts from James and his ma and the wheezes from his da and the flopping sound his body made as it fell again and again on the bloodied ground. There was blood under his head that splattered onto James's feet and pyjama bottoms whenever he was lifted and dropped back. His ma's forehead was streaked red where she'd wiped the sweat from it. James couldn't believe how sticky the blood was. Not like water, but thicker. And it moved slowly, even the splashes.

The sirens got closer and finally stopped, followed by the rattle of feet up the outside steps. The banging at the door and his ma shouting 'We can't move im!' and the voices beyond the door shouting 'Stand back!' and his da lying there all twisted and dead or half dead or something and the door breaking in on its hinges as the policeman shouldered his way through onto very nearly the very top of them and the ambulance men stumbling in over the broken door while the tears began to sting at his eyes and his ma saying, 'What's the point of fuckin greetin, at all?'

The policeman took James's hand and led him back up the stairs. James looked back down as the ambulance men straightened his da out, talking away to him all the time.

'Can you hear me pal?'

They whispered to each other, passing equipment between them and listening to his da's chest and shining a light into his eyes, the blue flashing light outside reflecting back off the door in the dark of the night, the policeman's voice coming into James's ears from under the mad confusing mess at the bottom of the stairs.

'Come on you wi me, son.'

A gentle bird-like voice. In the roar of everything that was chaos and sweat and urgency.

In the front room, the policeman sat James and his ma on the couch and knelt down in front of them. He had a nice face, took his hat off. His hair was greyer than his da's, and his neck bulged out over his shirt collar, reddening at the rim every time he moved his head. When he spoke to his ma, the policeman's nose bent at the tip; every time he spoke a word, a wee bend. It made James laugh and as soon as the laugh came out, he felt the tears well up from his stomach, from his toes. He couldn't stop them, and he felt ashamed and angry and when the policeman held his hands out to him, James punched them and slapped them and cried and cried, seeing nothing but blur, hearing nothing but his own tears. The policeman let his hands stay there, outstretched, taking the punches and slaps till James was worn out. His ma had left the room by the time he sat back into the couch.

Another policeman arrived. He whispered into the first policeman's ear and left.

His ma came back into the room with three cups of

tea and a plate of Rich Tea on a tray. She had cleaned the blood from her forehead.

'They've taken yir da to the hospital. We'll go and see him tomorrow.'

She handed a cup to the policeman and one of the biscuits to James. 'Go get changed out of those dirty clothes and get back into bed. Mind and wash yir feet.'

As he left into the hallway, James smelled the blood in the air, the light at the bottom of the stairs still on. He walked over and looked down. The door was propped against the wall of the outside steps and the floor was smeared with blood, streaks up each of the walls. He felt sick and ran to the toilet.

As he closed the toilet door, his ma shouted from her seat in the front room. 'Don't you be getting back up tonight, yi hear me!'

When he was back in bed, quiet in the dark, the two policemen came into his room. His ma stood behind them.

The policeman with the bendy nose came over to his bed. 'Did you see what happened to your daddy, son?'

James shook his head.

'Did you hear anything?'

James shook his head. He snuck himself further into the bed, under the soft warm of the blankets.

His ma stepped out from behind the second policeman. James didn't look at her. The first policeman smoothed his hand over James's newly cropped head.

'I hope your Daddy gets better, son.'

When they left, James drifted slowly back towards sleep, ebbing in and out of the pounding of his heart and the indecipherable noise of policemen speaking to his ma as she was seeing them out, the voice of Mrs. Henry, and his ma telling her in a half blur what had happened, and the sound eventually of her mopping and scrubbing the stairs. Singing a wee song,

Oh rowan tree, oh rowan tree,
you'll aye be dear to me...

In the morning, the sun sneaked into James's room through a gap in the curtain. His ma was standing over his bed when he woke. Her face was set.

'What will you say when people ask you what happened?'

James sat up out of his sleep and touched the wallpaper, feeling the roughness against his fingers, rubbed his eyes with the other hand.

'Eh?'

She repeated. 'What will you say?'

'Nuhin.'

His ma walked out into the hall and shouted back into his room.

'Ye'd better get up. We've ti get ti the hospital for eleven to meet the doctor. And see yir da.'

She shut the door over behind her.

James raised himself up, swung his legs round and onto the floor. His flannel pyjamas had pictures of Spiderman on them and were too small, the legs tightening round his thighs as he spun from the bed. They were his favourites. He'd another pair his Auntie Annie had got him for Christmas, the only time in three years he'd seen her, and they were sky blue with dark blue on the collar and cuffs. Boring.

He pulled the curtains back to reveal the sky and the roof of the house across the way, its chimney drifting smoke into the morning sun. He got dressed, pulling on everything he was wearing yesterday, even the pants; he didn't care, even though his ma would be mad if she found out.

He went into the hall and through to the toilet. He peed and washed his face and brushed his teeth, counting to a minute to make sure they were nice and clean. He liked the feeling of the toothbrush on his gums, scraping and sometimes nipping, but the taste of the minty toothpaste made him gag most mornings when it went down his throat. When he got a new toothbrush, he'd to brush more gently or the toothpaste would become pink with the blood from his gums.

He went into the kitchen. His ma was standing making porridge at the cooker.

'Sit down and eat this quick. We'll have ti go soon.'

She slopped the porridge into the bowl, then he added milk and started to scoop it up from the edges where it cooled quickly. He worked his way right round, turning the bowl to make it cooler as he went, then added more milk and started again. Round and round until he was finished.

His ma stood and ate at the sink, staring out of the window the whole time. He looked up at her between spoonfuls of porridge, the sun lightening her black hair, how she leaned into the sink, straining out of the window to catch something that was going on outside and she tutted and shook her head and slurped when she ate her porridge, which she always gave him a row for.

There was a chap at the door.

Mrs. Scobie's voice followed 'Are yi there Ellen?'

She came into the kitchen, wringing her hands.

She nodded to his ma. 'How're yi doin hen *smhhu*,' she said, then, 'Y'okay son *smhhu*' to James.

She plonked down at the table. She sniffed every time she spoke.

'Hope he's okay Ellen hen, *smhhu*. '

'Aye.' James's ma rattled a cup of tea onto the table and

handed Mrs. Scobie a plate with four fig rolls and three Rich Tea on it. Mrs. Scobie picked up a fig roll and dooked it into her tea. James glowered. They were his favourite and if she had another one he wouldn't get any. His ma and his da would never let him take the second last biscuit because that would be rude as it left only one on the plate. His ma took a fig roll and handed James a Rich Tea. He broke it in two, put one piece on the table and started to gnaw the broken edge of the other, scraping it up and down with his teeth, all the time listening to Mrs. Scobie asking questions about his da and sniffing and his ma answering like she couldn't be bothered with her.

He drifted into the night before, his da lying at the foot of the stairs and his ma and him pulling and hauling at him as he moaned broken air from his lungs, and the smell of blood and drink and the heaviness of his da.

Suddenly he felt his ma's hand hard on the back of his neck.

'Watch what you're doin wi that fuckin biscuit fur God's sake.'

And she hit him again on the hand, and the remnants of the Rich Tea scattered across the floor.

'Get that picked up right now.'

Mrs. Scobie tutted and sniffed. His ma slammed her tea onto the table and swept out of the kitchen as he was on his knees scraping Rich Tea crumbs up and into his mouth.

Mrs. Scobie looked over the table at him.

'You need to think more about yir ma son, *smhhu*. She's havin a hard time and you shouldnae be giein her trouble *smhhu.*'

They took the number 62 into the town. His ma usually talked to nearly everyone when she was on the bus, looking round her and moving her seat when someone else came on at Barrachnie Cross or the Shettleston Road. It always seemed to James like she was in some kind of whirl, different from in the house; like she kept all of herself for the bus, like it was her place. The way his woods were for him. Where he could be himself and nobody else would bother him, the high trees swaying in the wind, the quiet leaves of the ground elder and the nettles.

But today his ma was quiet. Three women got on at the stop after theirs and nodded to her. One of them put her hand on his ma's shoulder and said 'You okay, hen?' His ma gave a quick 'Aye fine,' but no more. The women sat two seats behind and that was all there was in the way of chat for the whole journey, till they got off at the Cross and headed up the High Street to the Royal.

It was a long walk up the hill from the big clock tower. The buildings glowered down at him as if they wanted to squeeze the air and the light out of him. His ma walked fast, the way she always did, with her face set like flint and the cold air rushing round her, and James had to keep half running to stay with her, the smell of the streets chasing him on.

The hospital was huge and dark and busy. When they entered the foyer, his ma let the door swing back onto him. It was heavy, with brass plates at his head height. Dulled with hand prints. He knew that a boy would get knocked off his feet easily if a nurse or someone didn't catch the door just as it hit him. The foyer was a massive circle, with people rushing through doors and standing in groups talking. The ceiling was nearly invisible, rising above the stairwell that edged its way round the walls and up and up, nurses and doctors and all sorts of people walking and limping and pushing and barging on the wide steps. James let his eye the follow ornate patterns of tiles on the floor to a blue star in the middle.

There was a strange yellow smell in the foyer, like a sweet bleach that clawed at him, half wrapped itself around him. As if it was trying to tell him it might be okay. Every time the doors swung open behind him, James could feel the outside air take some of the sweet yellow smell away into the streets and the smell of buses and dust coming in.

His ma went to a desk in the corner of the foyer and asked a man in a hat about the ward his da was in. She just had to tell the man the name of his da and when he came in and they were pointed up the stairs to Ward 19.

His ma said, 'Mon you,' and he followed, tripping after her.

The yellow smell was stronger in the room his da was in. James didn't like it at first and he tried to wriggle away till his ma glared at him.

'Wheessht you, sit still or I'll give yi one.'

But then it was as if the smell worked its way right into him, pushing past his nostrils and into his throat, through his hair and into the skin of his scalp, into his clothes and oozing inside every part of him. The smell lifted him as he watched his da in the bed, warming him. Cosy and clean and safe.

Most of his da's face was hidden beneath a huge bandage and he'd tubes everywhere. Nurses smiled at James as they came in and out. There were three other men in the room, all with visitors sitting quietly, looking at them, the same as him and his ma were doing.

His da said nothing, his eyes opening and closing slowly, his head turning back and forth all the time, only a tiny bit, as if he couldn't stop it. His ma sat on the side nearest the window and sorted things from her bag.

'Jean Henry sent yi this cake.'

She put it on the bedside table.

'Here's yesterday's paper.'

She smiled across to James when she said this, throwing the newspaper onto the foot of his da's bed.

James shuffled his seat nearer the bed and bumped the metal rails which ran along the side. 'Sorry Da,' but nothing back, only his da's head moving slowly one way and the other, his eyes opening and closing, opening and closing.

The tubes that came from under the blankets and out of his da's nose trailed down under the bed and up onto bags on stands or into the wall. One of them had watery red stuff at the bottom of a loop which moved slowly up and down. His da didn't seem to notice. His hands were laid neatly on top of the bedclothes down the side of his body. The one nearest James had a big bruise on the back of it. Occasionally the fingers twitched and James noticed that when the fingers twitched his da shut his eyes.

A nurse came in and nodded to his ma.

'Right you, mon,' his ma said.

She lifted her bag and walked quickly out of the room, saying 'Cheerio' to the man in the next bed. She said nothing to his da.

'See yi Da.' James shuffled round the back of the chair and past the nurse who smiled at him and rubbed her hand across his head. James dodged out of her way, anger welling in him. 'Leave me alone.' He snapped at her.

When he went out of the room, the yellow smell followed. He looked back at his da in the bed. His fingers twitched and his eyes closed.

The nurse said, 'The doctor can see you now,' to his ma.

She bent down to James, but this time didn't touch him. 'Just you sit there for a wee minute, son, and your mummy will be back soon.'

He sat on a chair against the wall in the corridor, the nurses bustling around him. He shut his eyes and let the noises of the ward and all the yellow smell drift around him. It was only a few minutes till his ma came back out of the doctor's room, her face set and her lips pursed.

'Mon you,' she said.

He followed her quickly to the top of the stairs and down into the foyer and out through the big dark door. She held it open for him and smiled down as the smell of the streets met him.

'We're goney be fine son.'

V: Maura, mother.

An intransigent sculpture. – Inspiration required. –
The dying and death of parents. – Cooking interrupted.
– An invitation refused.

MAURA STOOD AT THE DOOR of the shed, sweat drying on her face, the trickle of it cold on her back, the weight of the heavy face mask in her hand. James was over at the back door of the house with a Stihl saw, hunched over a slab of Caithness stone, carefully drawing the blade to create a groove for the real cut. His shirt lay over the fence and she watched the muscles flex on his back and shoulders as he carefully held the blade to the stone. Dust flew up around him as the saw cut in, swarming his whole body. The sun fought through the dust as it rose and swirled.

He turned the saw off. A sudden silence. He straightened up and laid the saw on the table, swept away the residue of the dust from the stone with his hand. As he turned, he took the paper mask from his mouth and waved it over at her.

'Want a coffee, pet?'

She shook her head, but then felt a sudden need for it and shouted back immediately. 'Okay then, you getting it?'

He laughed back over to her. 'Course, ya dafty, woundae offer yi a coffee and then get yi to make it yersel.'

She laughed too. 'Catch you in a minute. I'll just go and put the torches off.'

She walked back into the shed, now dark after the daylight outside. She put the mask down and adjusted the settings on the oxy torch before nudging the cables back against the legs of the bench with her foot. James always mocked her for her health and safety, but she knew how easy it was to have a stupid trip and take a finger off with one of her tools. Then what?

The floor was littered with shaped and welded metal. This commission was a small one by her standards these days; a bird for a private garden at Wiston. A bird that would hover beneath the heather and scree of Tinto Hill with the harriers and the buzzards and the ravens, a bird that would crush with its beak and rip and tear at anything that moved within its gaze, that would hunt at night and hunt at day and swirl in the sky against the dark side of the hill, the dark edge of Tinto, the dark-edged bleakness, the bleak dark nothingness of it. A steel bird rusting in the wet uplands, melding into the spare earth over hundreds of years, wind and rain softening it back into the earth, lifetimes after the lifetime of her.

When she first worked on the bird, she was in her shed for ten hours each day, shaping and cutting and setting the piece in motion. Then suddenly, it stopped. She couldn't even think what the bird would be, except a bird. But nothing living then. But, in the last three days, something had clicked and the steel had spoken to her. She'd made progress. And now this morning, when the rain had begun to scatter across the roof of the shed, it was all lost again. Nothing. She hardly knew why she'd carried on.

She walked round the slices of steel, in and out of them, brushing her foot against them.

James appeared at the door.

'You comin? Yir coffee's getting cold.'

'Okay dokey.'

She was glad he came in, felt lifted by his smile, his

wide gorgeous smile. She kissed him. Soft on the lips. Tasted his sweat. She was happy they were kissing again. She hated fighting with him.

It had come to a head the previous day. Maura and James hardly ever argued; there had never been any reason to, beyond the occasional niggle. In the small arguments, Maura rarely took James on; just let him blow it out. But this was different.

She knew she was to blame; it was her that was shifting the whole foundation of what they were together. She could hardly believe it herself, that she, of all people, was considering changing. The argument had started because of Sara, her thing about friends coming round. Maura had been torn, but James was intransigent. He wouldn't listen and Maura had to take a stand and make him hear her.

'You might be right, James, but that doesn't mean you shouldn't listen to me.'

'But ...'

'Don't.' She felt her hands clench. 'Listen to me.'

She saw a look in his eye; he knew that this was not a moment to be rash.

'I'm absolutely serious, James. We need to think carefully. I'm just not sure any more.'

She felt calm when she was talking to him. It was odd, because her whole inside was turning over. Everything she held close was slipping away.

He'd stepped back.

Now, they walked in silence back to the house, James in front of her, with his hand trailing behind him into hers, their fingers dancing with each other.

Maura kicked her big boots off into the back porch as

she passed, and breathed the warmth of the coffee from the kitchen into her lungs. She sat down opposite James in the seats by the French doors, the soft cushions eased into her back. She was used to bending and lifting when she was working, and her back was strong, but it was still nice to have a soft cushion. She put one leg onto his knee and sipped her coffee. She loved when he had his days off from the museum. Recently, he'd spent more and more time visiting his mum in hospital, but he was still there for Maura. She wondered when they would fix things after the big fight: a day was a long time to let things fester.

'When you going to see Ellen?' she asked, checking his face as she did so.

She worried that he was too calm about his mum's illness, as if her death was going to be harder for him than be for anyone else. Even though it was a normal thing.

'Pretty much now' He rubbed her toes through the thick sock. 'I'll get there before the mad rush. And not stay too long.'

'You take your time, love. I'll sort the dinner. There's lamb in the back porch.'

'How's the birdie comin on?'

'Mmm.' She hesitated, felt the well-known shift in her belly, felt James's finger squeeze her toe a bit harder, just when he asked the question. A tiny bit harder. She smiled up at him. She knew what she needed to do.

'Need some more inspiration,' she leaned nearer, 'lover.'

He kissed her, ran his hand along her leg, squeezed gently at the top of her thigh. Her tongue searched at his lips.

'That,' he leaned back, 'can be arranged.'

She felt warm inside. Calm.

'You've changed yir tune fae yesterday.'

He smiled at her. She didn't say anything.

'You okay, Maura?'

'Yes.'

He was staring into the distance. She kept looking, right in his face. He turned to her, smiled. She looked into his eyes and he looked back into her, deep down. Into the very heart of her.

She kissed him again. He pulled away, gently.

'I know we need to be careful, pet. No do anythin ti hurt Sara. But,' he hesitated, 'you need it, know what I mean?'

'I know. You're right. I do need it.'

They sat in silence for a while, the sun flitting in and out of the clouds, the tap of the wind on the back door, the smell of coffee and the distant sound of sheep, the soft stroke of his finger on her foot.

She thought about Ellen, lying in the bed in hospital for months, slowly ebbing away. James seemed to find it funny, ironic that such a fighter and basher and life-liver would be squeezed out of the world in a slow passing.

Maura's mum had cancer too. But hers was deadly and fast. Maura was still only twelve when it happened, six months after they'd found out. Her Dad had revived from the fat couch and seemed to float on the air after her mum died. Bits of the old him returned. Even at her mum's last moments and at the funeral, he was bigger and better and more alive than in all the years since Paul died. It was like he no longer had his crutch and he knew that if he didn't stand up straight he would fall down and never get back up.

Maura lived her teenage years in among his recovery, her mum and Paul hovering in the air like gas, seeping into her lungs and choking, her dad now commanding and visionary. As solid as the Devil's Arrows that stood at the edge of Boroughbridge.

While her dad grew into a coping man, Maura's life skipped past. She sped through school. Rushed between there and home and friends' houses. And the woods. Laughed and cried, hissed and spat, cowered and bit back like all her friends.

Maura's gran died a year after her mum. From then, Gramps and Aunt Joanne were always there for her dad and her. Like clocks ticking the same time in different rooms. Each safe and warm.

Everything else was safe and warm too. Even the one time John Wilkes tried to kiss her when she was fifteen. His beery breath as he fell over when she dodged his drunk advance. 'You stupid old man,' Maura told him. She didn't tell his wife or even her dad or Joanne, kept it between her and John Wilkes and stared him into a shiver every time he was near. She practised her stare on him. Perfected it.

Maura knew that the only thing that mattered was to be in charge. Of herself. Of other people. As she reached the end of school, her dad grew into his bubble and Maura grew into hers.

Then she found herself drifted away. Away from the blur of years. Away from her dad and the house and the street and the woods and everything that was Boroughbridge.

Even with the years at the Art School and meeting James and all that had happened, it seemed she was here all of a sudden, with James and Sara. Their life. Her dad had shared it for a while before he died, suddenly, in the living room. Where she and Sara had tried to revive him. She'd seen in her daughter at that moment what she had seen in James all those years ago: an unformed, vibrant spirit.

Maura had felt something inside herself too that she had rarely felt before: pity, pity for her dad, lying unalive on the floor and she and Sara worn out by the pressing of his chest and from blowing air into him. She had felt the same thing when Sara was born, that tiny spark of pity that she doused and doused and doused, but, sometimes, flickered, unquenched.

Both things were true: she loved her daughter, but she needed to create too.

And to create, she needed the inspiration she could only find with James, in what they did together. She'd begun to worry that those moments would kill their family, undo everything. The horror of being caught sometimes made her shudder. She imagined it all crashing round about their ears.

Sara weeping, in a corner, terrified, wailing. 'No Mum!' 'No Dad!'

Police cars.

Sara taken into care.

Maura thought about the baby on the beach in Dumbarton. Alone. They'd waited. They hadn't abandoned it to the waves.

The oystercatchers had squealed in the estuary wind.

This was the very first time she'd felt any spark of pity, for anyone.

There was only one thing that Maura could do. She needed the energy, the inspiration. Without all that, she could never have created what she did. Maybe just one more would be enough, would fill her up. Give her what she needed.

She turned to James. 'Love you.'

'Love you too pet.' He leaned across and kissed her. 'It'll be okay. Honest.'

She nestled into him, felt him squeeze her, strong and definite. She closed her eyes, rested there against his chest.

After a while, he said, 'I need to go. Get down there before the rain kicks in big time.'

Maura looked out of the window, across the field, the light clouds merging into grey and the sun disappeared, except for a hint, a smear of pale light.

When James left, Maura stood at the kitchen window, watching as the tail lights disappeared down the drive, the rain beginning to bounce noisily on the porch roof.

When James had a blow out, Maura knew it upset Sara, even though she seemed to let it wash over her. Those moments had been fine when it was just Maura and James, but when Sara came along it was if James didn't know how to deal with a child. He stumbled into fatherhood. Maura had shaped him up and he was fine. They talked about having other children, but Sara was enough. Too many mouths to feed. Too many to keep hushed.

Then Maura did get pregnant, when Sara was nine. James was shocked.

'I mean, pet, I'm no wantin rid of it or anything, but look at us. We not a bit old for all that again? Apart fae anythin else.'

Then it died. A tiny wee death. Hydrocephaly. Six months in, all the movement stopped.

Maura felt alone, her and this baby inside her. Waiting for the induction to scoop his life out, a drip, drip, drip. Then his tininess. This little thing that had nothing left to give after such a short few weeks of near-life.

They saw him, disfigured, blue-black, a nurse holding him in both her hands in a soft cloth.

Pity. She felt it then again. For herself.

'He's our boy Maura.'

'I know. He would have been beautiful.'

Maura rinsed the cups through and placed them on the drying rack. Two clinks. The rain on the window. The shiff of her socks on the tiled floor as she headed back for her boots.

In the shed, Maura picked up her mask and pulled the pipes and the oxy torch out from their resting place. She looked at the huge slice of steel and drew her breath. She so much wanted it to speak to her again, but it was nothing but a chunk of unfinished, unattractive metal, swinging gently from the block as she nudged it. She put the mask and the torch down and stood back from it. Nothing.

She walked round it slowly. The chain creaked as it returned to rest. She looked at the concave and convex sections she'd worked on earlier with such certainty, but now she couldn't see at all what it was she'd been trying to do. She held her breath right in and walked all the way round three times before she let it out. Still nothing. She rubbed her hands on the parts that were smoothed out and the rough parts that had been allowed to respond as they willed. She sat on her stool and stared at it.

After ten minutes of fruitless watching and looking and breathing, Maura stepped into the space beyond the main workshop to the smaller area at the back. She picked her way over to the wooden bench where a series of steel arcs lay like a chocolate orange newly split. She picked up each segment, examined it for how well it fitted to its neighbour and turned each to lie turtle-like on its back.

On the bench beside these were James's clocks, in varying degrees of readiness. He took the off-cuts from her sculptures and turned them into quirky timepieces. Twice a year, he loaded up the car and headed for a craft fair in Edinburgh. He usually sold the lot: angular polished shards; rusted, bashed flats; unshaped mild steel pieces; all with weird hands and set in bog oak or sandstone bases. She had recently become frustrated how easy it was for him to finish these tiny jobs, but the real issue was with her, not him.

'Bother,' she said out loud. She breathed calmly and slowly, turned and walked out into the rain, sliding the large grey door of the shed behind her.

It was quiet in the house, still only two-fifteen and an hour or more before Sara would arrive back from school. She could do something domestic until then, but even that felt beyond her. She slumped onto the long couch in the living room and closed her eyes.

The sound of footsteps running on the gravel drive woke her, and within seconds, Sara burst into the room. She yelled 'Hi Mum.' and sped past, thumped up the stairs.

Maura drew the necessary breath. She followed her up and into her chaotic bedroom.

'Bit late in, Sara.'

'I was talking to Emma at her road end.' She hesitated, unbuttoning her school shirt.

'She okay?'

'Yup.'

Sara fixed Maura with a gloomy smile. 'We're going to go to town on Saturday.'

The previous week, Sara with tears in her eyes despite her attempts at choking them back. 'But Mum, why can't she stay, she's my best friend and you always say no.' Head dramatically in her hands.

Maura had raised her eyes to James who was sitting in the easy chair at the window. A smile half on his lips that disappeared when Maura pursed hers. They both knew it was unfair, but there was really no way that could happen. No possibility, realistically. And Sara should have known that by now.

'Tell your friends it doesn't suit my work, Sara.'

At which point Sara was up, the tears now unleashed, the kitchen door slammed.

'You know she's always welcome to come round, 'Maura shouted after her,' Sara's feet stamping up the stairs, 'just not to stay...,' the bedroom door slammed, 'the night.'

Then blissful silence.

Thankfully, since then, it looked as if Sara had sorted it in her head, accepted it. She was a good kid. Sara was clearly fine if she was only talking to Emma at the road end and not pushing for more. Message understood.

She was half way changed in seconds, school clothes already discarded on the bed, her jogging bottoms on and a tartan shirt being squeezed over her thin frame. Sinewy.

'That's great, love' she said, 'do your homework and do not, I repeat, do not disturb me unless it is really, really important.' The words uttered in a slow staccato. 'I have a sore head and need some space. And I have to make the dinner. So please, do what I say.'

'Okay Mum.'

Maura clicked the door closed and headed back down to the kitchen. Silence. She would do better tomorrow. Tonight, she needed to get things sorted for the big bird. Needed a spark.

She picked the mobile phone from the floor and sat in

the sunny chair by the back kitchen window. She texted James.

how u?

Nearly immediately he came back

ok Ma even more no good.

She texted again

sorry x.

Then, from James

xx ☺

Maura replied

need inspiration

Nothing for a bit, then

goodie ☺ *xxxxxxxxx*

Maura slept again in the heat of the sun, her head at an awkward angle, and woke suddenly to another text.

Bk bout 8 will lk 4 inspiration ☺ *xx*

She felt the warmth of James's hand very nearly come through the phone and hold hers. She thought about the boy he was, and the strength she saw at once in his eyes. Saw the fight he had to be himself, and how he'd been true to that through all the years they had together.

She stood and walked over to the sink. She splashed water on her face, the cold immediately wakening her up. She dried herself and poured a glass of water, took a big slurp. 'Get a grip, girl', she said. Out loud. She, of all women knew what she needed to do and what she needed to be.

She looked at the text again, thought about those big slices of steel in her shed. She needed more than just herself; she needed James. He would bring her inspiration: only with him could she be whole, the same as only with her could he be whole.

She shut the curtains and picked the bag of Fir Apple

potatoes out from the cupboard. They were full of eyes, and beginning to go bad. The last time they'd planted this variety, they'd been fine, now it was just about impossible to clean in between the grooves and turns. Maybe they'd been left in too long, or the soil was too rich with the extra humus from the last time it was added. She smiled at that, how death is life, life is death.

She gave up on them, dug out a sack of Maris Pipers and started to peel them. It seemed a shame to eat bought ones when you had your own. Mind you, these were Davie Hill's, and everyone around held them as the best you could get. She'd bought them by the bag directly from the farm ever since they had moved up from Glasgow.

Sara shouted in the background from the living room.

'Muuum. That's me done it all!'

Maura didn't respond.

Waited.

No more noise.

Sometimes Sara disappeared to her room for hours, but it would be clear she was there from the bumps and bashes or *thump thump* of music. There was no sound now, which meant she'd gone outside. That was what she did. Went into the fields, sat by the river, floated in the big tyre or took the small kayak. Maura was the same at that age. Even before her mum died, she liked being on her own. Ever since Paul. In the woods, just being there. It made sense of everything else. She liked that about Sara, that she knew how to make sense of things, that everything could be unspoken, learned by osmosis.

Maura enjoyed cooking, especially when she was working like she'd been on this latest piece and getting nowhere fast. Hard work, welding and cutting and moving big pieces of steel, even with the block and tackle. James was always telling her to get help from someone, but he should know better than that. How would that work? She would be curtailed, stunted. And what would she do when the last burst was needed, if she needed to find that last bit of inspiration?

James usually did all the cooking when she was this busy. He came in from the museum on the days he was working and got on with it. He was a great cook. Her domestic goddess, she called him. He'd laugh and try to rugby tackle her onto the floor or the bed, but he usually ended up on the wrong side of that deal.

He was at the hospital three times a week for the last five months with Ellen. Maura wouldn't like to die in such a protracted way. She knew what a sudden death looked like of course, and that was preferable to months of dying. She liked the way her mum went too, with hardly a ripple. But Ellen was easing her way out of the world as if all the hassle she'd caused over the years was slowly washing out of her.

They'd taken Sara with them last week. Maura was surprised how easily she dealt with it, sat on the bed, talked to Ellen as if she were awake, laughed at the turn of her lip or the raise of her eyelid the few times they happened. That was maybe be the last time she would see her.

It was lamb tonight. Roasted with herbs and butter and pepper. And green beans. And these bloody potatoes. The lamb came from Alan on the farm next door, killed nice and young for a good taste. Maura liked that, looking out into his field at the lambs and eating them months later. It felt right.

The Maris Pipers were easier to de-eye. She cut them all into quarters put them into the pan to par-boil them before roasting. A little bit of salt.

It was raining outside and the window trickled with it. There was a leak in her workshop roof which had let an occasional drip onto her most of the afternoon. She usually found that kind of thing energising, *tip, tip, tip*, as if the air was part of her work. As if the whole earth was sculpting the piece with her.

She would get there. She always did, and one day this bird would fly among her other sculptures. She had major pieces all over: Glasgow, of course; London, Perugia, and Perpignan in the last four years; York; Edinburgh (*the reluctant émigré* she called it); a handful in smaller towns in Scotland and the north of England. And the one in Spokane. The last piece she finished was a bird too. It was already in place, rising into the sky between Sheffield city centre and Park Hill. It represented the symbiotic relationship between the city and the regeneration of an area that, only fifty years ago, was a regeneration itself. That was how she worded it in the spec after living in one of the un-resurrected flats there for a month to get the feel of the place: the feel of steel.

There was a time when she was nearly throwing her sculptures out the door of her workshop. She'd worked at such a fast rate, using all the energy she had from the last burst of inspiration.

'Calm down dear, it's only a commission,' James had said.

Then it stopped. Suddenly. All her creative energy emptied out. She needed re-filled. She resisted for so long, torn between her need to create and the love for Sara and the guilt that had grown in her over the fourteen years since she gave birth to her.

She was still working on her non-commissioned piece for Boroughbridge; six years and she still hadn't got it right yet. A piece for the woods and the Devil's Arrows and the memory of Paul and the trees and all of that. She wanted it to sit in line with the three monolithic stones;

she knew that her slab of steel would make sense of them in a way that archaeology or science never could. For the moment, it sat in the corner of the workshop, a metal monolith, ridged and dark. She went back to it time and again, nudged it towards what it would be. What it needed to be.

Her great love was the Clyde, everything it ever was, a moment, swept on in its forever rush. A wet jewel, it was the silver heart of the West of Scotland, Glasgow's antidote to the gristled motorways. Her first major work, unwelcome at first but now beloved as *The Gorbals Grannie*, had eaten its way into people's hearts. It had been her platform, the spring from which everything else flowed, the start of it all. From this, she had been catapulted to local, then national attention, then wider and deeper and bigger. Of course, what everyone else saw as the start was really more of a marking of her and James's first moment.

This bird that she was with now, this emerging thing of beauty and fire and steel and rust, had its doppelgänger spirit in the five-foot long egg, bent in fire and riveted. But it had lain for three weeks hardly touched, still, the embryonic soul of it un-born. It was waiting for what she and James could bring to it. The spark of something going out, the spark of something going in, lighting up her hands and her eyes, her heart and soul and fingers and sinews and singed skin and abraised, bashed arms. Inspiration.

This was what she needed for all her pieces, the essence she bathed in, poured on, drank, scooped, swallowed, slept with and dreamt in. Each piece that ventured uncontrolled into the world, on roadsides, in squares and gardens and galleries, overlooking parks and sea-sides and frontiers and rivers: every one of them had another, a soulfriend, the source of all its life and strength.

The bird would only be completed when the egg was. And the egg would only be finished when James and Maura found the spark.

That was what had really been at the root of their massive blow out the previous day; not just what Sara wanted, but the whole reason she could never get it. James was angrier than Maura had ever seen him.

'I don't know what the fuck you're on by the way. You're the one that always said ti be yirsel. Well you fuckin well be yirsel.'

Maura's heart beat loud, her fists clenching opened and closed. He was right. She knew it. But what was she to do?

'This could destroy the whole family, James. Maybe all this isn't worth that. For Sara. For you. Even for me.'

She'd placed her hands on the kitchen table, opened her fingers wide to calm herself down.

'Maybe we should just stop.'

He looked up at her from the chair. Shook his head.

'Do you really think that you could do that, Maura? Really?'

'Could you not? If need be?'

'No. I couldnae. I'm happy Maura. Needs fuckin must sometimes. Get it out. Get it fuckin out of ma heid. Cos see if I don't, I'll fuckin burst, man.'

He sat back in the chair, the sunlight soft on his hair. His face was set like flint, like Ellen's face. He was breathing hard. Maura saw the greying sides of his hair glisten in the light. She was nearer fifty than forty. Was she really prepared to give up her art? And everything that went with it? She watched James's jaw clench, the muscles in his face and neck tighten.

'I mean, you're the only thing that keeps me sane. But you and me, Maura, we're like one thing. Even without Sara. I love her, obviously, and I would never hurt her and I know we have ti be careful, but I couldnae stop. No completely. Wouldnae even be right. No for us.'

'I suppose.' Maura hesitated. 'You're right James. I just... .'

'I know.' He'd kissed her then, soft on the lips. 'But mind I need it too. It's no just you, Maura. Me too.'

Maura knew in her bones that today would be the day; that this very moment James was out there, in the real world.

'That's a joke,' James said when she called it that. 'What's more real: this or that? Them or us, Maura, eh? Them in the fuckin real world, man, they're nothin, fuck all, heehaw. Except what they are to you and me.'

He was out there now. Waiting.

She hoped.

The potatoes hissed and spat as boiled water spilled onto the hotplate. She moved the pot to the side till the water subsided, till it was a slow simmer.

She checked the temperature of the oven, then put the uncovered lamb in its steel tray onto the other hotplate, to sear the flavours in before roasting. It sizzled, sparking out herbs and fat. She shook the tray, turned the lamb over, more sparks and fat. The smell eased into her nose, swirled into her hair and round the room.

James was great with Sara, despite what he said. Even now with all her mood swings, and everything else that must surely follow, and her disappearing tricks all the time and *I hate this family* and *I hate you*. Typical teenager.

He'd walked out. Even when the argument subsided, he needed space. She knew that about him. He'd always been like that. Flare up, calm down, storm off, done. She watched him through the back window. He walked in and out of the sculptures in the field, touching each one with his hands as he passed. She loved his hands. Gentle, strong.

Maura looked up at the wall, smiled at the photograph of her and James in the crowd of a gig, a band on stage behind them, a small guy with glasses, wearing a skull and crossbones tee-shirt smiling beside them, and her and James staring straight into the camera, very nearly through the lens.

It hung next to the photograph of her dad, the one Sara had taken that first day he arrived. Not quite the man he'd been, but still a sparkle in his eyes as he reached out to Sara. Maura missed him. Thought about him often as the sun went down behind the hills in the far distance. And she always thought about how much her mum would have loved it here.

Her dad had faded away from the hulk of a man he had been to the gaunt man in the photo. He'd always been fat, ever since she could remember. Fat, when he had her and Paul running full tilt into his belly. Fat, sitting on the couch, depressed for years after Paul died. Fat, after her mum went, all his vigour forced back out of him to shield him from the pain of being alone.

On the shelf above the photographs were all the things that James and she had collected over the years since their first moment. They'd kept the red-haired guy's camera. She used it to photograph her work as it progressed in the shed. It seemed right.

Beside the camera, a round stone; she lifted it from the shelf and wiped the thin layer of dust from it. It was the size of her fist. James had used it on a woman's head in

Paisley one May evening, while she was out running with her dog in the fading light. It was their second moment: Barshaw Park, a quiet, peaceful place, looking down over the rows of sandstone houses. The runner woman's dog, a handsome collie, had tried to bite James, and Maura dealt with it. She kicked it in the ribs and it flailed for a second before rushing back towards James. What loyalty. But Maura had loyalty too and grabbed it by the neck, twisted the collar hard. Its owner likely saw this one last thing as she struggled in her garish yellow gear; Maura squeezing the breath from the dog, and James high-fiving her as he worked one last smack to the woman's head. Nothing stirred in the park then for what seem like an age as they lay back in the warm late sun.

Next, the rattle that was tied to the baby's pram in Dumbarton. Maura leaned up and took it from the shelf. Dust floated down after it. She blew. More dust spiralled into the air, disappeared as if it were never there. She shook the rattle, its blue and red blurring and the *shhkk shhkk shhkk shhkk shhkk* of the beads inside. Maura loved that sound. When Sara was born, James put the rattle above her cot. Maura swapped it for one her dad sent up from Boroughbridge with *I'm a little Yorkie* on the handle.

Down at the shore, the wind skittled along under the high scraggy cliffs where the tide of the Clyde estuary was far out and the sand was grey and muddy, the father face down in it, the squeal of an oystercatcher. That moment. She very nearly breathed her whole life away. A rush.

James wanted the dummy, but the baby was crying so hard that it had tugged Maura's heart a bit. She insisted that they hide along the shore till somebody came, just to make sure the baby was alright. She felt a whirl of unknown feelings. Sudden unsureness after years of certainty. Who wouldn't feel a tug when a baby cried?

She worried she was going soft till three days later she found out that she was pregnant with Sara. But it wasn't just that, not just the pang of motherhood nibbling away unknown inside her. From then she had felt less certain, less happy about what they did. What she needed to do. But what else *could* she do? Without the spark of inspiration, she was nothing as a sculptor. Would a fox be guilty feeding on a rabbit? Or a buzzard on a vole? Creating was like living: without it, life was nothing. The very air her soul needed.

And so, she kept on breathing.

More things: the pair of Red or Dead glasses (she smiled at that one every time she thought about it); a slate plaque with a seal on it from the house in Oban; the Mercedes car sign and the half empty bottle of Grouse from that frightening day they were nearly caught at Ingleston; the travel alarm clock with the blue trim, set still at 8.25; two identical signet rings with P and R engraved on them.

Underneath the shelf, telling the story of the years that went alongside all that, were more photographs of Sara and the three of them all together and some with her dad and some with Ellen.

There was a knock at the door.

'Hi Maura dear, you in!'

Marisa stuck her head round the door, followed, in a flurry of umbrella, by Josephine Tadstock, one of the horse people who had invaded the area over the last five years. Maura hated them all, their pretentions, their obviousness. 'Nothin a fuckin Tommy gun wouldn't sort out,' was James's comment when he saw any of them.

There were some horse lovers who had ponies in ramshackle sheds, on scraps of land, but most were not ordinary like that, most had paddocks and daughters to match their ostentation. They came around because she was well known. Nothing else.

'Come in, ladies.'

Marisa was a good enough neighbour. She rented Alan's farm cottage, lived on her own, and Maura worked to keep the balance between friendliness and distance. It would be a very bad thing to get too close.

James had no friends at all, except for Maura. That was how he liked it. Nothing to get tangled up. Nothing to lose or chose between. A family man.

Josephine brushed past Marisa as soon as they entered the kitchen.

'I've been talking,' she sped over to Maura, 'to the Community Council, Maura and we, well I, would like to talk to you about you exhibiting at the art show in the autumn.'

Maura smelled alcohol from her breath.

'Could you,' Josephine leered closer, 'see yourself to agreeing? Just this once? I know,' she sat herself down at the kitchen table, 'that you're not, well, inclined, but it would be such a help.'

She stretched out and put her hand on Maura's arm. Maura's muscles flexed involuntarily, but Josephine kept her hand there, smiling.

Marisa spoke up. 'I did say, Maura, that it wasn't really your thing, but it would, I suppose, be a bit of a coup. But don't feel any pressure, really.'

'Thanks Marisa.' Maura pulled her arm quickly from Josephine's grasp and stood up against the Aga. 'It really doesn't come easy to me, and to be honest, I would say no if you asked me a hundred times.'

Josephine sat quietly.

Marisa muttered, 'Totally understand, dear.'

Maura smiled. 'Now,' she said, reaching for the fig rolls from the cupboard, 'want some tea?'

VI: Sara, girl.

New lambs in old skins. – Great friends and a shit stupid guy. – What it is that makes us what we are. – Gramps and Nana and death and stuff. – An arrival.

SARA STOOD IN THE RAIN. The wind skelped her face and stung the ends of her ears, the smell of the wet air from the west racing into her.

She looked over to the house. The light from the back room glittered through the curtained windows and for a moment she thought she could hear her mum shouting. The wind played those kinds of tricks, and if her mum really wanted her the light at the back door would come on and flood the yard and she would be framed in the doorway.

Sara loved the dark. Even the gloaming, the half dark that smothered everything in grey. But it was the very very dark that she loved the most: the noisy dark when owls and cats and foxes crept and swept and screeched; when hedgehogs and rats and slugs snuffled and slimed and sniffed everything they could find.

The field was flat and ran all the way from the fence at the back end of the house to the river. The water's edge was meandery because the river ran on the flat earth and had to twist and turn like a worm to get along the carse to Stirling.

She let the wind beat the rain against her face; it trickled into her neck and down the inside of her jacket and tee-shirt. In the far distance, the last light was seeping away behind the mountains, and the sky had a grey-blue tinge. Even in the dark and wet, the sun left a stain on the day.

To the left of the house, the fruit trees were bent in the wind. Occasionally, a grunt or a cough from her four sheep emanated from the trees as they snuggled in to avoid the worst of it. Their neighbour Alan had given her them last year when she was helping with the lambing.

Alan knelt on the gravel, three dead lambs piled beside him. Their mouths clamped shut on life, their legs un-flexed.

'We've always been early sellers, Sara. Lots o ither folk go later, but we hit the market early and folk expect that, so they look oot for us.'

Sara didn't really care about all that. She was more in-terested in the actual lambs and the lambing.

Alan picked up the first of the dead new-borns. He skinned the feet, sliced up from the navel and around the face and then peeled the lamb's skin from its body, leav-ing a pink, almost human carcass.

He reached over to pick the first of the live new lambs from the pen he'd made from straw bales. It bleated and wriggled as he worked it round to start getting it into the new skin.

'Jist like shoochling a bairn into a baby-gro,' he said as he fought against the resistance.

Sara watched the lamb jerking and trying escape as Alan held it into his chest while kneeling. He was gentle and forceful at the same time. It gave her a warm feeling. The lamb sounded like her pal Emma's wee brother when he was getting his nappy changed. And his legs kicked just the same as the lamb's as it tried to pull out of the new skin.

Alan tossed the carcass of the lamb into the corner be-side the water butt. He placed the re-skinned lamb into another pen, where a ewe wandered slowly across and sniffed it. The lamb skiffled into a corner, still bleating and mewing, while the new mother followed it around, nudging it gently with her head.

He picked another dead lamb from the pile. The dogs watched him, sneaking slowly towards the discarded carcass. Moss, a red-coloured bitch, sat low on the ground beside the water butt, advancing slowly and stopping when Alan looked back at her. The other dog, Joe, a Border, tried the same when Alan was placing the next lamb in with its new mother. He threw a stone at him.

'Get, ya little fucker.'

Sara laughed

'Sorry, lass.'

She laughed again and he shook his head, smiling,

He skinned the next lamb, leaving the carcass beside him and picked out the third live lamb from the pen. As he began to wriggle it in, it bleated like it was being slaughtered, writhing even more than the first one.

'Little cunt, get fuckin in there.'

Alan struggled its feet into the legs of the skin.

Joe and Moss edged closer. Sara kept one eye on the lamb and one on the dogs as they snuck towards their prize. When Joe reached the carcass, he snatched it and dragged it back into the shadow of the shed. He ate it fast, and then vomited it into the corner, hoping Alan wouldn't see, vomiting and looking sideways to check. Moss fought for the vomited lamb, both dogs snapping at each other and nicking in to grab a piece of the half-chewed meat before skulking away and swallowing it down as fast as they could. Moss got a large piece down in one gulp before Alan shouted again. Both dogs disappeared behind the corner of the shed.

Sara walked over to the fence and her four sheep trundled

over, bleating in unison. She loved wrestling ewes to the ground for Alan to check them when they were struggling to give birth.

'Be careful not to hurt the mother or the lambs.'

And when she hesitated, 'Come on Sara, get in there, you need to give it enough welly to keep the yow from bucking too hard.'

She had to make sure Alan had a chance to get his hand into the ewe and check the lamb out. The ewe would always make a kind of *'phnnmyei!'* sound when he put his hand into and *'mmmynaa!'* when he came back out. A mix of surprise and pleasure, Sara thought. She was too embarrassed to say that to Alan, but she told her mum later and she said not to be so crude. Then she laughed and she told her dad and he laughed too. Her mum and her dad were quite cool really. They hardly ever gave her a hard time, especially about stuff like that. They always tried to make her feel happy about things, even things that she did wrong or couldn't understand.

They were like everybody else's parents in lots of ways, even though they were so different in others. Even if other people didn't know it. They would never really understand if they did.

She couldn't have friends round like other people, only occasionally. And never to stay of course. A lot of the other kids thought her parents were weird. They thought she was weird too. A few of her friends were really nice. Emma, Lucy, Amy and Scott. They stood up for her.

Earlier that day at school, in the first floor corridor, she'd heard a grating voice. 'Oot the way gawky weirdo.' John Taylor, laughing as he bumped into her, Sara's face suddenly flaming, the familiar tug in her stomach. She held herself back from launching at him, knocking him right over the balcony. She could very nearly see him, sprawled on the floor below in the foyer, that bitch from behind the desk running out to him, pupils and teachers appearing like flies around him. She knew she could. If she wanted.

Scott appeared suddenly, Emma following behind him. She stepped up to Taylor. 'Leave her alone, ya fuck.'

'Aye, dick.' Scott forced himself right into Taylor's face.

Scott had a wobbly hand he could do nothing with, but his other hand worked, and he was a better fighter with one than most boys with two. He'd battered Taylor the week before for calling him a spas.

Taylor backed off, turning to Sara as he left. 'Daft wee bitch.'

Sara knew not to bring trouble to the house, so she walked off with Emma and Scott. Smiled to herself. Her mum and dad would be able to sort Taylor easy. They were cool in ways that nobody, not even Emma, could ever guess.

The first time she knew, she'd broken the big rule. Snuck down late at night when she'd been warned.

'Not tonight Sara. Okay!'

She knew. From the look her dad gave her.

'Okay.'

Nothing more was said. This was how it always was. That rule, the only one that got the look that she knew meant real trouble. Until then she hadn't even the tiniest inclination to think about even imagining doing anything different than going to bed and going to sleep. Until that night, when the notion took her. Nearly by the hand, it took her, down the stairs.

Her heart beat high and loud in her chest. She heard voices.

A kind of crying.

'Leave me. Please.'

Sobbing too. Quieter.

'Leave me. Please.'

The sobbing was in behind the kitchen door, and scratching and bumping and the crying becoming louder.

'Leave me...'

'Would yi shut...'

Her dad's voice.

'...the fuck...'

Another bump and the sobbing stopped.

'...up!'

Sara was shaking. Her knees and arms were cold and jerked as she sat on the bottom stair. Listening.

The sobbing again. Just twice, and another bump.

Then her mum, 'You all right James?'

'Aye, the cunts.'

Another bump bashed the kitchen door. Sara froze. Then nothing.

A minute later there was the sound of heavy things dragged across the floor, the door into the back porch opening, the sound of panting. Silence.

Sara's heart was beating so fast she thought she would burst. She couldn't stop herself moving to the door and opening it slowly. In the middle of the kitchen was a smear of blood that led out into the back porch. And the sudden laugh of her mum from out there and her dad and a giggle from her mum and silence again.

Sara shut the door, her heartbeat filling her head. She snuck back up the stairs.

In the dark.

To sleep.

She'd understood it all gradually, let it sink in over the last two and a half years, listened to the night-time. Waited with baited breath for the next time her dad brought someone back to the house. She felt a swish run through her body every time she thought about it.

Sara walked down towards the edge of the field, squelching through the mud and the rain-softened grass. At the point she could see the night's reflection rise off the water, the noise of the river spilled into her ears.

From the other side, a squawk rose up into the darkness. She made out the brief white flash of an owl as it floated across the night. No sound from its wings and just the briefest ghost of a bird in the rain.

She loved her river, the Forth. Her mum's favourite was the Clyde. She'd made that big sculpture on the south bank, the one folk called *The Gorbals Grannie*. The first time Sara saw it, when she was still in primary, the statue towered above her, its face set over the river to the city, one hand in the air in a big fist, the other opened and out to the side, out to the west.

Her mum had said, 'Look, Sara, over there,' pointing to the opposite bank. There was another statue there, much smaller, a rusty steel woman with both her fists raised up into the sky.

'It's like they're sisters or something, Mum, yours and that other one.'

'That's La Passionara,' her dad had said. 'All to do wi the Spanish Civil War. They'll no teach yi that kind of stuff in school.'

Her mum laughed quietly, rubbed her dad's hair.

'No funny Maura. This is about strength, being what yi are.'

Sara watched her dad's face, then her mum's. They stared deeply into each other's eyes, without a smile, then leaned over her. Kissed, with Sara looking up, squeezed between their two bodies.

Sara had unveiled the one in Edinburgh, a giant twisting figure with no face. They stood on the hill overlooking the city and the Lady Provost shook her hand before giving her the scissors to cut the string that held the huge sheet on the statue. Sara had never seen it until the sheet undraped from the steel bulk. The drawings her mum had shown her and the scale model were nothing to this. Enormous. And beautiful. As the sheet slipped up and off the rusted steel body, the crowd of people shouted out and began to clap. Sara felt proud.

The field at the back of their house had a lot of her mum's sculptures in it. When Emma came round, she'd almost always want to go and look at them. It annoyed Sara sometimes, because Emma and her mum would talk away about sculpture and art and painting and all sorts of things and Sara wasn't really much good at that. Anyway, Emma was *her* friend.

Sara loved the sculptures too, but she preferred to look at them alone. Her bedroom window looked out over them to the river beyond and the fields and the mountains unfolding into the distance. The sculptures each sat on a concrete base on a raised piece of ground. In the dark night, she could just see the one that was nearest the river's edge. The Rock of the Birds, her mum called it. It was the only one made of stone, a huge black arch with a big column of sandstone about four feet in front of it.

'It's a cave, Sara.' Her mum took her hand that first day her dad had finished putting it in place, and led her to the mouth of the huge black arch. Through it, she could see the sandstone pillar rising up, a path of stone between the two. The top of the sandstone column had a hole through it.

Her mum stood with arms leaning on the pillars of the arch. 'At the solstice, the sun will shine through the hole and into the cave and all the fairies will come out and dance in the field.'

Sara's favourite was The Twins, the last one she made, two rusty steel people being sucked into the ground, their hands flailing, eyes wide and fearful. It was if there was something under there sucking them in, deeper and deeper. The Twins were near the house, down beside the rows of apple and pear and plum trees that ran in four lines from the back of the house to the river.

Alan was cheeky about her mum and dad. 'Who in their right mind plants trees on the east? You tell me that Sara. No protection fae the wind. And yir mither gibberin oan aboot the view ti the west. I like yir mither fine, ken, but she's a bit of a nut.'

He smiled over at her, looking, Sara knew, for a reaction.

Alan thought her folks were daft: 'hobby farmers,' he called them. Just because they'd a few sheep and some hens.

When she told him, her dad said 'The man's a fuckin arse.'

As Sara stood there on the edge of the river, the water sweeping past darkly below the high bank, she felt as if she could jump in and be swept away. She didn't know where she might end up. Perhaps in Iceland or Norway eventually. Perhaps stuck on a branch half a mile downstream beside the half-rotten carcass of a sheep. She felt a bit disgusted when she thought about the smell; nothing worse than the smell of something dead that's on the turn. It was always best to get things buried quickly.

Sometimes she and Emma would come down to the river in the early summer, when the water was low and eased along lazily. They'd get a couple of old tractor inner tubes and float along, spinning each other round and round and talking about things.

Other times, Sara would go on her own and spin below the muddy banks. The air was always full of the sounds of insects and birds, the baa of sheep rising from the fields, dogs barking, the occasional burr of a tractor or a quad, the sploosh of the water on the muddy edges of the bank, the soft whisper of the wind in her ears. Swirling in the river, doing nothing. Hiding from everything else.

That was what was good about the dark; it was even better than the river for hiding. She'd often come out into the field in the night-time and stand in between the sculptures and imagine that she was a sculpture too. The figures would be hardly visible around her, all stood on their mounds of earth, present even if she couldn't see them. She could stand there for as long as she liked, pretending to be dead and made of rusted steel, the cold night air eating at her. Her mum faced all the sculptures to the west. It meant that if Sara was on the other side of the field, or in the field next to it that her dad used for potatoes, she would see them all staring at her, or just beyond her to the hills. The two that were not figures, the Rock of the Birds and the one that looked like a tree, were down nearer the river and it seemed almost as if they'd grown out of the bank. There were eleven altogether. Each on its own mound of earth.

Each one, her mum said, a memory.

When it was dark, Sara sometimes got a fright when the automatic light came on at the back of the house and illuminated The Twins. Even though she knew to expect it, their contorted faces would leap out of the dark in the sudden brightness and seem to be clutching at her from the other side of the fence in their desperation to escape from whatever it was that was dragging them into the earth.

Sara had watched her mum making The Twins. It was soon after that first night in the kitchen and Sara had wanted to talk to her even more since then. She knew instinctively not to mention what she'd overheard. Sara hadn't been allowed into the big shed before that. Her mum told her it was to do with safety, but Sara knew it was really because her mum wanted to be on her own while she was working. But she let her in when she started The Twins. She said it would be good for them to get some girly time.

'What's this one called Mum?'

'I don't rightly know, pet ... The Twins?'

She'd smiled at Sara. Her thin smile.

'Why?'

'Not sure, love.'

She stood back from the tangled metal shapes.

'Just feels right, I suppose.'

Her mum moved beside her, put her arm around her shoulder. A strong squeeze.

That was the start of the summer when they were still in primary school. Sara had heard Emma and some of the other girls in her class talking about girly time with their mums; but that usually meant going shopping for clothes or shoes and having a hot chocolate in a café in the shopping centre. For her it was donning welding masks and holding sheets of steel while her mum cut them with a torch. They drank Irn Bru in the mornings and water in the afternoons because her mum said they needed the sugar early and their systems cleared out later on. Nobody else was there except the two of them.

When The Twins was finished, Sara had helped bolt it onto the concrete slab her dad had laid the week before.

'Right, pet,' her mum said, 'just...'

She swung The Twins on the block over the holes she had drilled in the concrete base.

'... lower ...'

She pushed the whole structure inch by inch.

'... lower ...'

Sara finally let the metal down into place.

It was the best summer ever.

The Twins wasn't for sale: none of the sculptures in their field was. Sometimes people would come to look at other pieces her mum was making or to talk about a commission, and Sara would get to show them round the field after they'd finished in the big shed. Her mum always refused to sell, no matter what the offer was.

Sara walked over towards The Rock of the Birds. She came to the big sandstone pillar first. As she stepped up onto the concrete base, a hedgehog scurried through the black cave. Hedgehogs looked funny when they were running; hitched their skirts up, mumbling to themselves. Sara held her hand out to the sandstone and felt its roughness against her skin. It warmed when she touched it. She held her face against the stone too and gave the pillar a hug.

She hugged trees when they all went for a walk as a family into the woods. Her mum and her dad would run about chasing each other, laughing. Her mum was really good at climbing trees. Whenever they played hide and seek, it was nearly impossible to find her because she would climb away high up and sit quietly there for ages. Sara and her dad could get into the lower branches but didn't like going too much higher. They'd look up and up and up at her mum way high in the tree. Disappearing into the green.

Her dad's favourite tree was one on the high road up to Callander, a few hundred feet across a scraggy piece of field and looking back down over the slopes and across the flat of Flanders Moss to the hills beyond. He took her there last autumn. They made a picnic and cycled to the gate into the field, where they abandoned the bikes. They headed across the mucky, marshy land, aiming for a line of trees in the distance, leading down alongside a broken stone wall that separated the field from a forestry plantation. Some of the big trees had fallen down, and their limbs lay like dinosaur bones, blanched and broken under the trees that were still standing. Sara and her dad walked among them, looking up into the browning leaves and climbing on the dead bones.

Sara clambered up on a massive fallen beech and walked along its length; as she went, she was higher and higher off the ground and towards the end, when she was six feet up, the tree began to swivel down towards the earth, like she was walking on a see-saw and had stepped over the middle. She found she could control the huge tree by stepping from one side of the tipping point to the other. Like she could control the whole world with her legs.

'Some girl, by the way,' her dad shouted. 'Brilliant balance.'

When she reached the end, the tree lowered itself towards the ground and she jumped down into the soft mud. Her dad had a shot too and nearly got as far as she did when the same thing began to happen. She climbed up and they tried to do it together, but the tree twisted as it tilted and they struggled to stay on, grabbed a hold of each other as they began to lose their balance. They played on the tree for ages and laughed at each other falling off into the muddy earth below.

After about half an hour, her dad said, 'I've somethin ti show yi Sara.' He led her to the second last tree on the line, a huge one that towered above the others. Its branches were spread out in such a way, that she found it almost impossible not to jump onto the lowest one and scramble higher. They were evenly spaced and easy to move on. She looked down occasionally as she went higher, and saw her dad smiling up at her. Then he climbed the branches too and they were sitting there, a branch apart, looking all around. She'd never been so high in a tree before.

'This is ma favourite one,' he said. 'I pure love this tree.'

The land below them fell away steeply and Sara felt like she was floating above the world. She wasn't scared at all.

In the distance, cattle and sheep wandered slowly, and newly harvested fields patched the landscape. Bales of straw were dotted around and the whole land was spotted with farmhouses. The village beyond the first expanse of fields was a strip of houses, smoke rising from chimneys and settling slowly into a drift above the line of roofs. Then, the land flattened, and the whole carse had the look of a seascape. Sara could occasionally see the glint of a lorry or the sun bouncing off the windows of a car on the far road, the one that ran near her house. She couldn't pick their house out, but knew that it was on the far side of the river, just before the land rose steeply again to the Gargunnock and Fintry Hills. Beyond the flat tops of those hills was Glasgow.

'Can you see the house, Sara?' said her dad.

She scanned the view again, squinting into the evening light. 'No.'

'I think it's down beyond those trees to the left.' He pointed down through the village. 'Yi see Thornhill?'

She nodded.

'Right, keep yir eye on the line of trees on the hills beyond that. Yi got it?'

'Uhuh.' She wasn't sure, but she uhuhed anyway.

'See it now? Just getting the chimneys?'

Sara strained her eyes. 'Not sure.'

'I think I can see yir mum skivin out the back wi a coffee.'

'Ha ha, Dad, very funny.'

He was like that, always making jokes.

They sat for ages before her dad handed her a roll and cheese and her flask of warm blackcurrant juice. When they'd finished, she wandered off on her own for a bit, round through the wood, swinging on the see-saw tree again and back till she landed at the base of the big beech.

Her dad was still sitting in the branches, his eyes closed. Sara looked up at him for a moment. She felt warm. Even though she knew there was something really bad about him, she felt safe. He could make anything okay. Sort any problem. She knew that. She felt strong when he was there.

She walked over to the edge of the slope and found a pattern of rocks that made a huge chair. She sat down on the flat stone and leaned back.

A plane flew overhead leaving a scratch of vapour on the sky. A buzzard squealed. Rabbits flashed across from whins to burrows. The wind blew gently round her.

Being with her dad there, she was the queen of everything.

Sara reached her arms as far as she could round the sandstone pillar. Near the top of it, her mum had carved a Celtic bird shape that interlinked with a snake, repeated round the entire column. Sara followed the bird and snake shape round the stone, as if she were dancing with it. She was amazed how her mum could keep things so even. Her friend Scott was good at that too. He had an accurate hand that never seemed to waver, his good hand. His wobbly hand was rubbish of course, but his good hand was maybe even the best hand ever.

Sara walked in through the arch. Sometimes she imagined she'd end up in a different world or in a different time, like the Lion, the Witch and the Wardrobe. Perhaps she'd be the only survivor of some terrible tragedy and she'd have to look after herself and try to find other people that had survived too. She'd have to go into the house and find the bodies of her mum and her dad, and that would be the hardest thing of all. She made herself cry thinking about that sometimes; but she liked to do it because in a strange way it made her feel good.

There was a clatter from the direction of the house. Sara stepped into the centre of the arch and craned her neck to see what it was. No movement. Only the wind bending the ends of the branches on the fruit trees and the faint flutter of a piece of orange plastic tape that her dad had wound round some metal poles where he had been digging that morning. Another hole that he didn't want her to fall into. It must have been the lid off the feeder for the hens or one of her mum's metal sheets that had been left outside; she usually worked in steel, but sometimes she used aluminium, and that was lighter.

One time a gust of wind caught a sheet of aluminium and it had lifted into the fruit trees. One of them was damaged so badly, her dad had to dig it out and replace it. He was mad at her mum for that and they had a big fight, him going on and on and on about Sara being hurt and her mum just working away quietly, not rising to it, not getting involved. That always made her dad even worse and he'd shout and bawl and stomp about till he calmed down. Sara found it funny and her mum would wink at her when her dad was flying off the handle like that. And that made her feel better. Her dad always apologised for shouting, and would sweep her mum into his arms and run around the kitchen table shouting, 'I love yowwww- wwww,' howling like a wolf and laughing and saying what an idiot he'd been for getting all upset like that. 'Sorry Maura. Sorry ma wee pet lamb!'

That was what arguments were like.

Sara knew her parents would never split up. She asked her dad once, not for any reason really, just to find out.

'It would be like losing an arm,' he said. He looked at her right in the eyes. 'Your mum and I are like one person Sara. Nothing can ever stop us, or keep us from each other.'

Sara had felt happy and frightened at the same time. Happy safe and happy frightened.

Emma's dad left three years ago with a woman from Chile he'd met at a pub quiz in Glasgow. Emma called her the cold bitch from Chile, which Sara thought was funny the first time she heard it, but wished she wouldn't keep going on about it. Emma's mum was horrible and always shouted at her, even when Sara was there. Some things are better kept behind closed doors. Emma was never as happy after her dad left, but she tried to keep it hidden from people by being cheery and jolly all the time. Sara could see through all that.

Sometimes, on nights like this one, when the wind blew like a mad thing from the wet west, Sara would look back to the small light from the house when she was standing at the river or in the fields beyond and feel a warmth burn right into her, a spear of heat from the house. Heat from her mum and dad.

She stepped all the way through the stone arch. Nothing happened. She looked across at the house again. There was still no sign of what had caused the noise, just the branches of the fruit trees swishing about in the wind and the light of the house flicking through them.

She stepped off the stone plinth and walked over to the edge of the river. She knew the path so well that she could walk all the way along the bank with her eyes closed if she wanted to. Every step had etched into her mind over years and years. Even when bits of the bank were washed away by the river when it was swollen, she knew the new line the first time she walked it.

The rain eased and the wind picked up. It carried the smell of the night with it, a nearly sweet smell at this time of year that was filled with yellows and blues.

She'd read on Facebook about people that could smell colours. Her dad said it was rubbish.

'Load of shite, Sara, don't let them play with your head, pet.'

He said that about on-line anything.

Sara knew he was probably right, but she believed the thing about smells, had started to make herself do it. The smell of scones was light brown and the smell of a wet dog was blue. The smell of a dead sheep was purpley green. The river whispered to her, trundling and gurgling along beside her. It smelt deep dark red.

When her gramps stayed with them, he used to smell of urine; not all the time, just in the weeks before he died. Before that he smelt of patchouli, the almost bitter perfume lingering on him at all times.

She loved her gramps. He only stayed with them for a short time and for most of that he sat in the couch in the sitting room or on the chair in the corner of the kitchen. He laughed and sang songs and told her she was 'the best thing since sliced bread' or 'as fly as a badger's cat'.

He always said he was having a heart attack. Sara remembered her mum getting annoyed at him. 'One day we'll ignore that, Dad, and it will be true'.

One day it was true. Sara came in from school, her last week in primary, and kissed her mum in the kitchen as she was sitting with a coffee and the plans of a new sculpture. A pot of soup was bubbling on the hob, the smell of chicken and carrots swirling round the room in a steamy haze.

Sara had tried to save him. She tried and tried and tried, but it was too late.

The sitting room door was ajar. Through the gap, Sara had seen his leg twitching on the floor. She pushed as hard as she could to make a space big enough to squeeze through, shouting 'Mum! Mum! Mum!'

She pushed and squeezed, till she fell into the room, in and over him. Her gramps was sweating and his face was grey, his legs twitching as he tried to catch his breath. Sara's hands were flapping and she was trying to think what to do.

She shouted, even louder, 'Muuuuuuum!

Her gramps's eyes rolled in his head, the breath of him snatched and fast.

Then he stopped breathing, his face grey and blue.

'Mum! Help!'

Her mum was at the door, shouting to open it and Sara was pulling at her gramps's legs, trying to make space. Her hands were suddenly firm and strong and her mum squeezed into the room, white-faced for a second before falling down beside him, feeling his pulse, whispering, 'It's okay Dad, I've got you. Ssshh. It's okay.' She pumped and pumped and pumped at his chest with one hand on top of the other.

Sara watched; her own hands were jelly again, needing a firm purpose like life saving or door opening.

Her mum threw her the mobile.

'Phone an ambulance Sara. Quick.'

She made the call, remembered everything she should say. She sat down beside her gramps. Her mum pumped at his chest.

'They're coming.'

'You do this now,' her mum said, 'and I'll do his breathing.'

Without thinking, Sara started, pressing as if her own life was slipping away. Her mum breathed the kiss of life into him.

And suddenly she stopped. 'He's dead, pet.'

Stopped.

Her mum pulled Sara's hands away from her gramps's chest and held them close to her own, squeezed them into her breast. Tight.

Then her mum let her go and stroked the side of her gramps's face. 'My poor dad.' And she lay onto him. 'Ssshh.'

Sara was shaking, the tears stinging, her heart beating hard.

Her gramps's face still as a tree in the silent air.

Her mum lying on his chest. 'Ssshh.'

Nothing. For a moment. Of nothingness.

After, they both stood and looked at him lying on the floor. His belly stuck out through his unbuttoned shirt.

Her mum bent down and buttoned the shirt over him.

'I remember we used to run onto that belly, when it was much bigger. Like a big friendly pillow.'

She kissed his forehead.

The sound of a siren in the distance.

Sara bent down and kissed him too.

Sara never cried about anything after that. Not even now, in the field, in the rain, where it wouldn't even be seen.

Her dad had said, 'Life is changed not ended.'

Sara liked that. But she wondered how it changed. Was he in the air? She could be breathing him in right then at the side of the river in the dark; although, with the wind, he could be half way round the world and she could be breathing in bits of other people. That was a horrible thought.

So she liked to think that it was the earth that Gramps was in, feeding plants, seeping into the river, some of him spreading out into the sea and on round the cold northern coasts.

They'd buried him under a huge slab of unsculpted granite. She looked across to the far side of the big shed where it stood alone, the lichens and mosses that clung to it shining just a little in the soft light from the house.

She heard the noise of tyres crunching on the gravel. She ran along the field and round the side of the house to see if it was her dad home. He'd been visiting her nana in hospital. She'd been ill for ages, but even before that she hardly ever came to their house. Sara didn't love her like she loved her gramps. She wasn't soft like him. Every time her dad came home from seeing her in the hospital, Sara thought he might say her nana had died too.

She reached the corner of the house just as the car eased to a halt in the gravel. When her dad opened his door, the light fell on the face of a young man sitting in the passenger seat. He had big dark eyes, and he was smiling out of the window into the night. Sara eased herself back into the shadows, keeping her eyes all the time on the visitor. Her dad went round to the passenger door and opened it, took a huge rucksack out and led the young man towards the light of the porch.

Sara stood with her back to the rough wall of the house for a moment, then crept round to the back door. As she went through, she heard the welcomes to the visitor, a hitch-hiker her dad had picked up wet on the road. It was a long time since he'd brought a hitch-hiker home.

And there he was, in Sara's house, his big dark eyes still clear to her from the glimpse she had of them. She stole quietly up the stairs to her bedroom. She wanted to change, to get herself together. She needed to look her best.

VII: James, father

Waiting for death. – A blast from the past. – Why
mothers exist. – Departure expedited. – Coming of age.

JAMES SQUEEZED THE BLUE alcoholic gel at the
door of the ward. He did it automatically, following
the pattern on the poster: rubbed his palms together, in
between the fingers, round and round the thumbs and
wiped them together again. Repeated it.

The gel had a smell that sliced into him, then disappeared. As if it never was.

His ma lay in the dim of the single room. The angle-
poise lamp seeped gloomy light onto her face, slid onto
the bedclothes, turned to grey stooriness in the corners
and in the shadows.

The room was quiet. The soft click and shift of the
morphine pump every so often, the *beep beep* of monitors
flashing their numbers. Her breath wasn't smooth, but
snatched briefly every twenty seconds or so:

nothing, nothing, nothing, then

Hih

in went the air, spilling into her, settling into her lungs,
then out in a low long

Haaaah.

Feet stepped past the room at intervals. The muffled
chat of the nurses and doctors at their station. The low
background sounds of a radio. A vehicle two floors below
on the entrance road.

He reached into his Lidl bag and took out the get well
cards. He placed them on the foot of the bed, before stuff-
ing the bag into his pocket. He took his jacket off and
placed it over the back of the chair.

Hih

He looked over to her.

Haaaah.

She lay with her hands outside the sheets, a tube coming out from under the left arm of the nightdress and up into the collection of wires and other tubes that ran in and out of the machines on the stand beside the bed.

'How you doin, Ma?'

Hih

'Still rainin out there. They keep sayin it's goney clear up, but they're talkin shite as usual.'

The monitor said *beep beep*, then nothing. A pale orange light blinking.

Haaaah.

'Right then.'

He picked the cards up from the foot of the bed.

'Here's all the news. Quite a few the day. Paddy Moran, he that pal of ma Da's? Anyway, him and Rita say they're thinkin about yi. Praying for yi. Good fuckin luck wi that, eh?'

Hih

'It's this one wi Saint Anthony on it.'

He held it towards her, then placed it on the broad window sill in front of the others. Saint Anthony, in a brown cloak, cooried the baby Jesus in his arms, a bunch of white lilies in the foreground.

Haaaah.

'Rena Mackay sent you one wi a lade on it.'

He looked at her for a reaction.

'A lade, Ma. Fucksake, eh?'

He hid Rena Mackay's card behind Saint Anthony.

He thumbed through the others. They were mostly flowers with a cheery message scrolled across the front in a diagonal, expanded style, designed no doubt to be jaunty and up-beat. Others had water: one beach and two with a burn running through woods, the trees the colour of ash in springtime, light and opaque and hopeful.

James imagined what it would be like if the greetings were honest.

We know you won't make it, but we're thinking about you. That would be okay.

We heard you were ill, don't want to visit, but need to keep up appearances. Honest, if dispiriting.

Hurry up and die. A bit brutal, but at least it would clarify things.

Get well soon did not mean *we hope you don't die*, but might mean *we quite like you and if you do die, then …*

She'd a lot of cards and James could never really understand why. Very few people had come in to see her, but the cards keep coming every week, usually posted through the letter box of her flat after morning Mass.

'Here's another one Ma. Belter. Michael and Anne Mc-Pake – hope to see you up and about soon. Maybe get a wee voddy in the Thistle.'

Hih

His ma lay still. Nothing. The *beep beep*, the green light.

'A wee voddy in the Thistle, eh?'

He laughed.

The greyness lifted for a second from the corners of the room and settled again.

Silent.

Haaaah.

'I think your voddy days are well behind yi, Ma. Sorry ti say.'

He sat down onto the soft easy chair at the far side of the bed. He adjusted the pillow behind him and closed his eyes.

Hih

He opened them, the green light flashed. His ma's mouth made no movement as she expelled her breath.

Haaaah.

He stood and picked up the jug of water from the bedside cabinet, poured some into a glass and took a drink. He wet the end of a cloth and dabbed the drying edges of his ma's mouth. She moved her jaw slowly.

Hih

He wet the cloth again and wiped round her cheeks and forehead.

Haaaah.

The door of the room opened, spilling the buzz of the ward in with it. A small, circular woman sped in, tutting as her bag caught the door handle. She pulled a couple of times and snapped, 'Would you not give me a hand here, James.'

By the time he was over to her, she'd separated the bag from the door and pushed past him to his ma's bedside.

'Oh, Jesus, Mary and Joseph.' She crossed herself and mumbled quiet prayers, her eyes to the floor.

Hih

When she stopped and looked over, James said, 'Hi Marie. How are you?'

She tutted.

Haaaah.

Marie had been his teacher in primary school. She nearly shaded his ma in the sharp biting she could do, her face ever ready to whip into a snarl, eyes that bore into him like a drill. She had a nose that was sharp and tight. She looked older than his ma, even though they were the same age. She smelled of dryness and her face was compacted with foundation. She reminded him, almost every time he saw her, of when she belted him or sent him out the class or otherwise pinned him down as a child. For her, it was a badge of honour to be disliked, and, even all these years on, she'd little else to offer. Her and his ma were great pals from the Chapel.

She greeted him with all the cold distance she could muster as she sidled round the bed, smoothing out the edges of the sheets.

'Your mother looks comfortable at least.'

She took her stare from the bed to him and back again.

'You'll be needing a break, I suppose.'

'No thanks, I'll be fine. I had somethin ti eat just a wee while ...

'... nonsense, off you go and I'll stay here.'

Before he could think, he was in the corridor to the nurses' station and out into the main concourse, heading for a coffee at the canteen.

His ma would have withered Marie with a look or a word, a barbed refusal to do anything she didn't want to. No matter how much he was like his ma in other ways, he'd never mastered that, the verbal stab in the neck. He'd found his own way and it was better than aping somebody else. His way would sort that bloody Marie. Bitch. Maybe not though. Best not mix business and pleasure. In any case, a coffee would be good, so James was as happy to go as daft Marie was to be rid of him.

He fished two coins from his pocket as he pushed through the swing doors into the canteen. £1.20 for a drink. The machine gurgled for a minute, then poured dark coffee and froth together into a cardboard cup.

He found a seat by the window that overlooked the cemetery. Cappuccino from a machine was normally plastic, but this tasted very nearly like the real stuff. He sat back and looked around the room.

The young Asian doctor from the ward nodded over to him. He was carrying a meal on a yellow plastic tray and a copy of the *The Sun* under his arm. He sat at the table three away from James and flicked the pages over from the back. He didn't look up, just read the paper and shovelled what looked like stovies into his mouth.

The froth on the cappuccino started to solidify round the rim of the cup, browning as it hardened, like his ma's lips. James smelled the coffee and took another sip. It reminded him of the warm sun at the lake in Italy.

He had swung out from the beach-front chalet at 7.30 a.m., cycling along the tracks through woodland and alongside the water to Garda and on to Bardolino. Marbled streets at the harbour side, beautiful people swinging perfect hips in the Sunday morning sunshine. The cafés were already busy by 8.30, the first tourists, like him, taking a well-earned rest.

A woman in a blue dress appeared among the tables. She was bright and beautiful and it was almost as if she'd shouted *look at me!* into his face. Shame that beauty was so transient, could be so easily destroyed.

She sat at the table opposite, her face turned to the lake. The sun glistened the sweat on her back. As she drank her coffee, the muscles on her neck twitched, a pulse beating slowly. James looked beyond her to the boats in the harbour, clinking in the rise and fall of the water. He could pick out Sirmione on the finger of land on the southern part of the lake. He swept up the hills on the other side. The green of the Parco dell'Alto Garda reminded him of the Trossachs and the hills near home.

He drained his coffee and closed his eyes. The heat of the sun.

The woman scraped her chair and James opened his

eyes again to see her walk back down towards the woods. He followed her slowly with his eyes. He stood, put coins in the saucer and walked over to where his bike was, against wall of the café. He pushed the bike down to the lake side and breathed in the air before setting off.

The morning sun warmed his bare arms as he cycled back through the woods, glimpsing the flashes of blue ahead of him as he caught her up.

James's phone beeped. A text from Maura.

how u.

He typed.

ok Ma even more no good.

She came back quickly.

sorry x.

He looked out of the window to the graveyard. He hated fighting with her, but she'd been the one in the wrong. Not carrying on. Fuck. After everything she'd said to him over the years. *Be yourself.* He knew she couldn't stop anyway. It was even more part of her than him.

He texted back.

xx ☺

He closed his eyes. Another beep.

need inspiration

He smiled. She knew he was right. They just needed to be careful.

He texted back.

goodie ☺ *xxxxxxxxx*

He waited for a minute, imagining Maura in the house. Nothing came back. He laughed and said 'Brilliant.'

The flashes of blue through the lakeside woods were like fish in a river, weaving seductive patterns, not knowing what would happen next, what might be just ahead.

James always liked the feeling that gave him, when he was ready to pounce. Sometimes he would take it to the edge. Right to the very edge. And then do nothing. And only he and Maura knew how close that was. Sometimes they stalked for a week and then stopped. Almost as good. But not enough really, in the end.

As he cycled past the blue dress, she turned to him and smiled. He smiled back. *Buon giorno's* exchanged. And on through the woods.

He typed again. *Bk bout 8 will lk 4 inspiration* ☺ *xx*

An urge to get back to his ma took him and he pushed his seat back against the wall. The young Asian doctor started at the crash that the seat made and looked over to James, nodded at him again and then returned to his paper. James put the coffee cup into the bin and headed back to the ward.

When he got there, Marie was just getting her coat on.

'I thought you were never coming back,' she said. 'I have to go.'

He wished he could throw her out of the window.

'Thanks very much for coming. Ma ma will have appreciated it.' Polite. It was a good thing to be polite.

He settled into the seat with the pillow in it and almost immediately was lulled into the uneasy rhythm of the morphine pump and the

Hih

Haaah.

Soothed.

When he was younger, he'd never have dealt so calmly with Marie and everyone else around who dragged him down.

But that was before he met Maura; she'd changed everything for him.

Life had turned out great. Her first three big sculptural commissions had set them on the road to the countryside. The perfect place. Peace and quiet to work, she told everybody, but he knew what she really meant. Work. It was funny to think of it like that.

James missed the city of course. The bustle. The opportunities. The way you could hide yourself in the streets. Dark corners.

Maura had stolen the limelight twenty years before with her huge sculpture on the south of the Clyde. Across from La Passionara, Love and Justice rose twenty-four feet of steel with her right fist raised like Dolores to the river and the other hand sweeping West in a welcome to all. Her face rose to the sky in defiance and hope. Glasgow was changing and Maura had played her part, feted by other artists and talked about in the political scene. A woman of profile was what she became, but not what she wanted. They nicknamed Love and Justice *The Gorbals Grannie*.

That was why they moved to the country, close enough to be near the city when need be, but far enough away that they could hide and be themselves. Be yourself: Maura had been telling that him all the years he had known her and he was convinced she was right. She was herself. No problem. He used to believe that old lie about it being nice to be nice, and he'd tried to be good, but he knew now that it was even more important to be realistic. Everyone had their different, individual limits. James knew what his were. That was why he was mad at Maura for trying to pull them back. From being what they really were. Together. He was angry at her, but also frightened that, if she couldn't stick in, he would be lost; he needed her.

Maura had painted a mural in Sara's room as soon as

she started to read. A clifftop. Somebody standing there looking down. Below it:

know thyself

Hih
She who bore him.
Fed him, slapped him, kept the heat in and the cold out, watched out for him.
Haaah.

His ma never really cared about what other people thought. She taught James to be the same.

'What would you be worried about what they think?'

And a fierce look that cut right into him.

When his da was still around, that was when she worried about what people thought. James remembered her with a sore face his da had given her and she wouldn't go out of the house till the bruises had faded. His da one minute apologising and following her around like a dog, and the next, threatening to 'fuckin gie yi another one, ya cunt.'

His ma always sent James to the shops for her when his da marked her face. He'd rush round as quick as he could, the handles on the two bags digging into his hands, hurrying back to make sure his da hadn't hit her again. She made him put the money in his shoe in case someone tried to steal it. Rattling back to the house with the change in his shoe, coins digging into his toes.

Sara had none of that. Maura's success meant they were well enough off. And the thought of him lifting his hand to Maura: it just wouldn't happen. And even if he did, she would slice it off.

He looked over to his ma in the bed.

Hih

Her translucent skin. The neat white covers tucked carefully up to her chin. She used to come into his room at night, when he was in the half sleeping place and tuck the covers up to his chin like that, smooth them round his shoulders, make sure they weren't over his mouth. She didn't say anything, just sorted the covers.

Haaah.

He had taken Sara up to see her the previous week. She stood at the end of the bed looking at this unalive person breathing her last few days. James wasn't one hundred percent sure how Sara would react, but he knew it was important to face up to things. She did, without any bother, though she'd never seen this version of death: drawn out, languid, unfinished.

'Why's Nana's face so yellow?'

'It's just the light, don't worry about it.'

James saw a tear welling in Sara's eye.

No drama or resolution in a slow death. Just waiting and thinking everything through.

When they were leaving, she leaned over and took his ma's hand, pressing it to her face softly.

'Later Nana.'

Now it was just him. He preferred that, if he was honest. The two of them in the near silence of the room.

Time to go. He eased out of the soft chair and looked down at his ma's face. Nothing but the

Hih

The soft comforting machine noises.

The quiet light.

The easy smell of cleanness.

Haaah.

He turned away. 'See yi in a couple of days, Ma.'

As he reached the door at very nearly the end of the corridor, one of the nurses from the ward came through it. She triggered the electronic opening with her jauntiness. A smile at the door and it opened wide to let her through, and she stepped from the cold of the car park into the bright warmth.

'Hya,' she smiled at him.

She was beautiful, shiny, young. And she really meant Hya.

It made him feel kind of good for a moment.

Then that dull heaviness in his belly, the ache in his guts as it worked its way through.

She talked to him about his ma, kindly. She perked up when he visited. And she may pull through. At least for a while.

'She's very strong. There's something... well just something about her.'

But she couldn't know anything about how strong his ma was, or anything else about what she did or could do or would do.

All the time, with her sweet icing lips moving and her doughy words bouncing out and around him and her nice shiny face blurring in front of him.

In the toilets at the Lewis's store in Glasgow when James was thirteen, a man standing at the urinal. He looked round when James went in, gave a half smile, his face lined and grey, a smile laced with something.

The urinal was one of the big metal ones, and it had the wee blue blocks in it that James would chase up and down with his pee if he was there by himself.

When he started to pee, the man moved over towards him. James edged away and peed harder to get it over quickly and the man said, 'You okay wee man?'

James was thinking, 'not really,' but, 'Aye, okay,' was what he said.

The man didn't even have his willie out. He was rattling change inside his pocket, his hand moving up and down.

chink chink chink chink chink

'I'm great too,' he said, and he moved towards James, his hand still in his pocket. He smiled at him and looked down at his pee. James's heart was beating mad and he was so far over there was nowhere left to go.

chink chink chink chink chink

He thought that if he swore at him, the man might get mad or something, so he just finished as quick as he could and ran out without even washing his hands. That was a thing he never did.

His ma knew as soon as he came out into the store. She was good at sensing. She made him tell her.

With his ma he never knew what was coming next; there were times when she startled him, times when she made him soar like a bird.

She went into the toilet, nearly taking the door down as she went. Her whole face concentrated in her pursed lips, her cheeks paled and pinched. James could feel the coldness flying off her.

Nothing for a minute.

Then she came out again and walked right past him without saying a word, straight into the stairwell and headed down.

She didn't tell him to go in, but he did. Automatic pilot. The man was lying in the corner, half against the urinal. Blood was seeping onto the floor and a large pair of scissors was sticking out of his groin. The ones with the yellow handles from their own kitchen. He was breathing heavily and didn't look up till James moved closer.

'Help me.'

James stood and looked at him. The man had one hand around the scissors. His other hand was on the rim of the urinal, trying to keep himself from sliding down further. James thought it was disgusting that his hand was in the urinal where everyone else had been peeing.

He liked seeing him lying there with his ma's best kitchen scissors sticking out of him. He wondered if his ma had got him right in the willie. She'd been cutting up bacon for the tea the previous night with them, and here they were, stuck in that man's leg.

He was wearing light green trousers and the blood looked like it could be any kind of stain till it dripped onto the floor and oozed along the cracks in the tiles, red and greasy.

When James walked towards him, the man reached his pishy hand out to him. James stepped back, keeping enough distance to get a good look, but not get caught. The man's grey hair was sweaty at the edges and his breathing was quick and snatched. James laughed because he sounded like a sheep at a farm near where he went on holiday one time that had its head stuck in a fence by its horns. When he'd tried to free it, it had struggled and writhed. It took him ages, and all the time it was bucking and making that same breathing noise. When he did set it free, it ran off, kicking its back legs in the air. *Baaaing* and dancing.

'Help me,' the man said again, this time trying to pull at the scissors, but only managing to hurt himself more. His face tightened with the pain.

James edged over to him, and as soon as he was near, the man grabbed out again with the pishy hand. James jinked away, and the man fell onto the floor.

'God allfuckinmighty. Would yi no just go and get somebody.'

But James wasn't going to do that. He could hear his ma's voice swishing, first a distant *wissi wiss wissiwissaa*, then louder, bigger, a swarm of noise crawling into him, filling every space in his head. He reached down, grabbed the yellow handles of the scissors and pulled them out. The man fell to the ground before he could grab him, fingers splayed in pain.

James didn't bother to look round as he washed the scissors and then his hands and left. Just heard him whimper, as the toilet door closed behind him.

The nurse put her arm out to comfort him, touched his shoulder, the warm press of her hand through his jersey.

'Your mother's lucky to have you,' she said, her shiny face blurring in front of him.

He could try his luck and take her home.

Imagine that.

But she wasn't right.

And it was too public, with cameras everywhere. It was harder to be secret than it used to be, but over the years he'd remained good at being unseen. He always chose carefully, and nobody had ever put the pieces together. He wouldn't let this nurse spoil that.

The electronic door hissed open and he was out of the bright warmth into the dark chill of the night.

It was one of those days. Where he knew that things were going to happen. That something was going to appear in front of him and the rest would take care of itself. A day with a soul of its own.

The journey home from the hospital often went in a blur.

Out of the city, onto the motorway, off the motorway, onto the long road, into the track to the house.

Tonight, James was focussed on everything. The particular orangeness of the street lights around the hospital, the way the ticket machine grabbed his ticket then his credit card, the timing of the red to red and orange to green at the exit of the hospital grounds, the sweep of the motorway's bends as the roads merged as he headed north, the way the cars nearly danced as they found their lanes, the huge rusty blueness of the gas containers at Blochairn, the girdered beauty of the railway bridge over the M80, every small thing at the side of the road, the first spots of rain on the windscreen, the sudden coldness as it began to bucket down.

The rain swept him through Cumbernauld. The figure of Arria rose above the road, its metal shine illuminated in purple and green. Maura hated it. The last time they drove to Glasgow together she had ranted. 'No emotional energy. Nothing.'

He took the first turn to Stirling and headed over past Saint Ninians and King's Park and out onto the long stretch of Dumbarton Road. Quiet on such a night.

The hitch-hiker was standing half a mile out of the town, just as the road narrowed after the bridge over the motorway. He appeared in the distance as a gatepost till James got closer to him. A car overtook him and lit the hitch-hiker up as it swept past, ignoring his outstretched thumb and hopeful smile. That smile. Big and wide and young. Nobody else on the road now but the two of them. For that moment.

Picking up hitch-hikers had become a habit. All those mad people from all over the world who were willing to stand at the side of the road and take a lift from a complete stranger. And the offer of hospitality.

Mostly, the next morning, if they'd taken the kind offer to stay, they were leaving for the next part of their journey. All the Scottish ones for sure. *Don't shite on your own doorstep.* James and Maura always offered them the use of the phone to let the folks back home know where they were. Sometimes they refused that: a good sign. Dislocated.

James stopped. Rolled the window down. Smiled out at the hitch-hiker as he ran, bedraggled, lugging his giant red rucksack to the car.

When he was nineteen, James hitch-hiked to Manchester. His ma had a cousin there and he felt the need to get out of Glasgow. All the whirring madnesses were spiralling around his head after John the counsellor guy had wandered in and pointed him in the direction that got him lost. It was the start of him trying to be good. Before Maura sorted him out.

It took him three hours to get to Lockerbie where he pitched up at a truck stop. He tucked in to the all-day breakfast and a couple of pints of dark beer and got talking to a big tall trucker who offered a lift to Trafford Park. Perfect.

Later, the road muddled the beer and the breakfast into sleep. His feet on the wide front shelf, rucksack at the door, the radio weaving in and out of his dreams. He woke up slowly into the half sleep before consciousness. He felt the driver's hand groping him. James kept his eyes closed, the driver's hand on his crotch, praying he wouldn't get a hard on. He started suddenly, as if only just awake, mumbled out, 'What the...' and the lorry driver pulled his hand away.

'Nearly there, mate. Just about off the slip to Trafford.'

James slowed his thoughts, heard John's voice, *stay*

inside the hula hoop, and he sat up, the lorry driver looking straight ahead, his face reddened, his long hair sweated at the edges.

'Thanks.'

He said nothing else.

John would have been pleased with him.

'Where are you from?' James said to the hitch-hiker, carefully, him being obviously foreign.

'Slovakia.'

'Ah, Bratislava.' He nodded, no clue where that had come from or anything, just out, automatic.

'No. Kosice. In the east.'

The hitch-hiker's dark eyes had a fullness to them. Perhaps a touch forlorn, far from home, but full of expectation. Hope.

'I am looking-g for the youth hostel.'

He swept his hand through the black hair that the rain had flattened against his head.

It was easy from there. James told him the hostel was far away and insisted he come home to eat a meal with his wife and daughter. They would love to meet a Slovakian and he could phone the hostel from the house to make sure that they had a bed. James would drive him there later.

So there he was bumping up the dirt track like a hunter-gatherer, a Slovak in the passenger seat. Leading him into the porch to meet the bright light and the warm smile of his wife, that he kissed

slowly

and the heat of the kitchen running out the door to meet him, the Slovak standing in the porch squinting in the light and the brightness of his wife. Not knowing what was coming next.

Inspiration.

The smell. Wonderful from the kitchen. Lamb something, herby and fatty, the smell of fat and herbs and lamb mingling with the excited talk in the porch and the Slovak standing, waiting to be told what to do.

In a flurry of jackets and boots, rucksack, sleeping mat, rain dripping all ways, the smell of Slovakian sweat mixing with Scottish sweat and a lamb dinner, they were out of the outdoor things and into the kitchen, the hitch-hiker standing on the tiled floor looking around the room, the photographs on the ochre walls, the Aga with pots chirping away, the huge table that could sit thirteen with ease, onions and garlic hanging in well-formed bunches above it. He rubbed his arms warmly and smiled at the family one by one.

'This is my wife, Maura,' said James.

She held her hand out so beautifully for him, smiled gently. 'You are so welcome.'

And then Sara, arriving in from the hall as they spoke. She was wearing a tight black top that hugged her shape, and red denims that James had never seen before.

The hitch-hiker stretched his hand to Sara.

'I am so very happy to make your acquaintance'

She smiled at the Slovak.

'Hi, what's your name?'

'Filip. And you?'

'Sara.'

Filip blushed. 'We have a goat at my home that we call Sara.'

A sweet, lingering grin on his face.

Sara laughed and Filip laughed, and in a minute, with the ice cracked, they were round the big table, and the wine open, and James suddenly remembered something.

'I've got some Slovakian beer somewhere.'

He scrabbled about in the back porch and held it high as he came back into the kitchen.

'Here we are: Starapromen.'

'Czech.' Filip said with a simple, almost beautiful, smile, and Maura joshed James for it, and the young man lowered his head the way that boys do with a crush on their teacher. Sara did the *duhuh* thing, and Filip looked at her quizzically.

And James saw that Sara had her eye on him.

That was the thing really. It wasn't just bringing a stranger into the house, to savour some Scottish hospitality. He was introducing something else into the dynamic. Tonight could have gone like this:

> sitting down after a lamb dinner
> kissing his wife on the warm smile
> coorying into his daughter coorying in
> music in the dark corner of the room
> the smell of herbs and the taste of lamb
> all greasy and tasty
> in the hours into the night.

But here they were with a Slovak. And a fourteen-year-old daughter with her eye on him. And everything else that would now inevitably follow.

'Tell us about your home town, Filip,' said Maura, as she handed him a plate with roast lamb and carrots on it.

Potatoes were passed round the table in the big dish. Filip spooned some onto his plate, rolling them beside the lamb and the carrots. He wiped his hands on his trousers, looked at the space between the top of their heads and the ceiling as if he were trying to read the answer and said, 'Not so beautiful as Stirling-g, I think.'

Coy.

'Kosice is a little larger, without a castle, but we have our Andrassy Palace which is also beautiful in the centre of the city.'

He left for a moment to the porch, then returned with a small daysack and fumbled a leather folder from inside it. He drew out a number of photographs and a brochure and placed them one by one on the table.

He beamed at the tiled roofs and crumbled walls of the town, and the smiling faces of his mother and brother and three younger sisters who were still at school and wore red dresses, and his brother worked as a blacksmith with his uncle who had been like their father since he died when Filip was ten years old in the road with a car coming too fast around the corner, no-one seeing who was the driver and the town mourning as if their own father and husband and son it had been who had died. The flowers in big vats by the doorstep where his mother, younger and thinner than you might imagine, looked straight into the camera, straight out of the photograph into the kitchen where they all sat listening to Filip tell the story of his family, of heat and work and the Velvet Revolution. The Andrassy Palace sat on the front of the brochure, neo-Baroque gargoyles leering from the corner turret, a family strolling among the gardened edge of it, strolling in the quiet sunshine across to the streets beyond.

'It's a very beautiful place,' said Maura.

Filip beamed again and sat back in the chair.

'Thank you.'

He put a potato into his mouth and smiled round at everyone for a moment, then gathered the photographs together and shuffled them back into the leather folder.

'Would you like?' He handed the brochure to Sara, KOSICE emblazoned proudly across the front.

'Thank you.' She took it onto her knee under the table, glancing through it.

James caught Maura's eye and knew they were both thinking the same thing. Sara had never had a boyfriend, and now was not the time to start.

Sara rose slowly. 'Thank you, Filip.'

She stretched out, yawned to the ceiling, arms just a little back like a swan in the second before lift-off, onto her toes, chin up and back to the surface in a splashless touch of heel.

Sara exited with the brochure in hand, her first trophy it could be said.

The rest of them sat for a moment in the smell of lamb and buttered carrots. Nothing was said. Filip coughed and straightened in his chair, James in his, Maura in hers.

James and Maura tried to be relaxed about all of this, that when Sara got to a certain age she would stretch herself, make decisions, take moments when they arise, fill the space they had tended for her all those years, and fill it as big as he and Maura had filled theirs.

Filip seemed to shrink a bit. His space shrank a bit.

Sara reappeared at the door. Filip looked at her, swept his hand across his cheek, then mashed a potato in gravy and put it into his mouth.

They talked easily through the lamb, the smell wafting round the kitchen with the conversation.

When everyone had finished, Sara began to collect the plates. James went into the back porch, rummaged in the freezer and found a tub of lemon sorbet.

As soon as he'd put the sorbet on the table, Sara arrived back from clattering the dishes into the sink.

'I'll have some then.' And bounced onto her chair.

Filip smiled over to her. She ignored him.

James smiled too. Glanced to Maura who played with

her spoonful of sorbet on her top lip before sucking it into her mouth. The pulse on her neck beating.

James poured the water into the cafetiere. Nice and strong.

'You not tired, Sara?'

'No.'

'Well think about it, pet.'

She folded her arms tightly and sat back in the chair.

Filip kept his head down.

Sara pushed her chair up and barged out to hallway.

James watched Maura follow Sara out with her eyes, then move them back to the table.

'Tell us about the weather in Slovakia, Filip.'

Sara barged back through again and out into the back porch, the door to the outside slamming hard behind her.

James shook his head. 'Teenagers, eh.'

'She seems like a lovely girl,' said Filip.

'She is.'

James had to get her out of the way. This was what Maura was talking about, the reality of family life.

They shared Slovak and Scottish stories. Maura told him about Boroughbridge. Filip soaked in everything she said.

Half an hour passed.

And then Sara came back, her moment, with a garden fork. She strode behind Filip, unseen by him, and thrust the fork through the space in the chair into the small of his back. She was a strong girl.

James's thoughts flashed to her helping Alan with the lambing, even at the age of ten wrestling ewes to the grass to let the farmer get a good look at them, happy to tangle on the ground with the legs kicking out and the horns, no fear, the ewe bleating and writhing and Sara holding on not saying a word. Just being in charge.

So the fork stuck right in, and Sara gave the handle a twist as it reached its limit. A moment of nothing. Then Filip broke it with something Slovakian.

James's heart was racing. No point in trying to stop her. He looked to Maura who seemed as aghast as he was. How did she know?

Filip looked at Maura too, her soft smile still there, his eyes trying desperately to locate safety, assistance, an explanation.

He looked at James. James smiled back at him, did the hunchy shoulder thing and raised eyebrow thing at the same time, which no doubt meant the same in Slovakian as it did in English.

Sara pushed the handle of the fork again and Filip gave out a yelp.

She still didn't say a word. The hint of a smile. She raised her foot to the fork, drew it back, then gave an almighty kick with her heel. Like she was digging potatoes. Filip grabbed at the table in pain, a low whine from his belly. He tried to stand, but the fork made it impossible for him to move beyond a crouch as it lifted the chair when he straightened. Sara gave another kick and he screamed.

He looked across at James again and shouted. 'Stop her. Please. Stop her.'

James was amazed he could still think to speak English at such a time. Admirable really. He looked straight at the Slovak and laughed.

What could he do but laugh?

Because it was funny. As if he would.

James looked into Sara's face. The smile. His wee girl.

Filip's breath was becoming broken.

Maura stood and walked round to the other side of the table, staring into Filip's eyes the whole time. Filip watched her till she was half way round, then Sara twisted the fork out of his back. He folded onto the floor, shuffled back, hands and feet scratching into the corner. He leant his back against the large sideboard, against the warm wood. Closed his eyes.

Maura took Sara into her arms, squeezed her tight against her.

Sara looked at the prongs of the fork, then up towards James. She looked straight through him. As if he were not there.

Maura reached Filip, and he opened his eyes again. He tried to stand but couldn't manage, slithering back against the sideboard. Maura bent down, lifted her hand to his cheek and stroked it. He cried, trying to hold her close, like a mother.

Maura looked up at Sara and nodded, then stepped away.

James stood up to get a better look.

Filip was breathing in bursts. He looked up at Maura, looked to Sara who was holding the fork aloft.

She thrust it into his chest.

The disbelief on his face.

Sara looked across at James. Into his eyes. She leaned on the fork and smiled a wide smile.

By the time the light crept through the clouds the next morning, James was shuttering the area around freshly dug earth, the concrete ready to be poured. In the big shed, he could hear Maura's arc light sparking new and frantic shapes for the Wiston bird.

Sara slept.

Two oystercatchers speared the sky, flying low in the

early light. Their *wheep wheep* split the silence. James looked up for a second, then continued hammering.

The wind hummed softly in the trees.

Acknowledgements

To Live With What You Are emerged from two short stories published in consecutive New Writing Scotland anthologies: *Random Acts of Kindness* in *Lunch at Yes* (NWS 20 ed. Hamish Whyte, Moira Burgess, Kevin MacNeil) and *Coming of Age* in *Milking the Haggis* (NWS 21 ed. Hamish Whyte, Valerie Thornton, Maoilios Caimbeul).

A number of friends and family members read sections and versions of the novel as it came together. I'd like to thank Joan Gracie, John Tracey, Pauline Healy, Neil Aitkenhead, Gordon McLure and Bob Marshall for giving me the confidence to keep nudging it into the Rejectosphere. (I'll not tell you how many times it bounced back.)

I'm very grateful to fellow writers from Stirling Writers Group who encouraged me over many years. Particular mention goes to Laura Fyfe, Neil Cocker, Carolyn Choudhary and Vicki Clifford for key support at crucial times. Deep thanks to long-term tutors Magi Gibson and Chris Powici.

Thanks to the G2 Writers who helped me get the discipline sorted, and for being great readers as well as great writers. A shout out to the G2 Big Sub group where I got the first half of this book properly together at last.

I appreciate being offered a place in 2014 on the Scottish Book Trust's mentoring programme. The novelist Zoë Strachan was my mentor and she guided me through the craft of telling a story over a whole novel. This book wasn't what I was working on then, but everything I learned with Zoë went into finally bringing it together.

Thanks to a number of writer friends who have been kind enough, at different times, to give me focussed support and the gift of critical honesty: the aforementioned Magi Gibson for helping me see what a serious writer needs to be about; Frances Sessford for clarity about the words and a sharp eye; Donal McLaughlin for insistence on getting the detail right and for his generosity near the end of the process. Thanks, too, to the superb Irish sculptor Brendan McGloin for help with technical bits along the way.

I acknowledge with gratitude the support of Sally Evans and Ian King who published my first poetry collection, *Good Morning*, with diehard publishers.

Gratitude too to Sheila Wakefield for agreeing to publish *To Live With What You Are* with Red Squirrel Press's literary fiction imprint, Postbox Press. Thanks to the Scottish Writers' Centre who brought me and Sheila together. It was great to have the chance to work with Colin Will as editor and to benefit from Gerry Cambridge's excellent design and typesetting experience. It has been a pleasure to be involved with Sheila, with her artistic momentum and her belief in this novel.

A NOTE ON THE TYPE

The inner text of this book is set in Miller, designed by
Matthew Carter and released in 1997. It is a 'Scotch
Roman', and follows the original style in having both
roman and italic small capitals. The style was developed
from types cut by Richard Austin between 1810 and
1820 at the Edinburgh type foundries of Alexander
Wilson and William Miller. Miller is a soundly
practical text face with an unexpectedly decorative but
unobtrusive italic.